LIFEGIVER

Publisher's Cataloging-in-Publication Data
Names: Hern, Edgar J., author.
Title: Lifegiver / by Edgar J. Hern.
Description: Includes bibliographical references. | Las Vegas, NV: KDP Publishing, 2025.
Identifiers: LCCN: 2025905104 | ISBN: 979-8-9928840-8-1 (paperback) | 979-8-9928840-9-8 (ebook)
Subjects: LCSH Psychic ability--Fiction. | Shopping malls--Fiction. | Paranormal fiction. | Science fiction. | BISAC FICTION / Science Fiction / General | FICTION / Fantasy / Paranormal
Classification: LCC PS3608 .E76 L54 2025 | DDC 813.6--dc23

LIFEGIVER

EDGAR J. HERN

LIFEGIVER

In the cold vastness of space, there is a star-forming region in the Perseus spiral arm of the Milky Way galaxy known as W30H. There, red giants and yellow dwarfs celebrate the birth of a new star. Within the swirling clouds of gas and dust, hydrogen nuclei are crammed together. Collisions among atoms heat the cloud until hydrogen fuses into helium, unleashing energy as light, marking the star's awakening. Star systems are bound together by gravity, and the distance between them ensures a birth without complications.

The fledgling star was born too close to a red giant, triggering turbulence. The intense gravity between them created a Roche lobe through which material from the red giant flowed into the evolving star. Highly concentrated hydrogen, along with carbon, nitrogen, and aluminum, ignited a violent nova in the ill-fated star, dispersing star stuff into space. Debris raced through interstellar space over millions of light-years, where the gravitational pull of neighboring stars captured most of these fragments. One such fragment was cast into the path of a white dwarf star.

The boulder hurtled through a spherical assemblage of comets known as the Oort Cloud. It sailed into a solar system, passing through an asteroid belt toward the third planet. The chunk of rock streaked across the sky at thirty miles per second, breaking up in the Earth's atmosphere over the Atlantic Ocean. By the time it sliced through the mesosphere, it had dwindled to little more than flakes of dust, a fraction of a micron, wafting like dandelion seeds. Gentle winds nudged one flake westerly over the shores of Miami, altering its course southwest over a shorefront park ringed by skyscrapers.

Wednesday, July 13, 1966.

Kevin knew he was carrying too much but kept going. When he reached the pushcart, the stack of books leaned like the Tower of Pisa before it toppled to the floor with a resounding thud and a flutter of pages. Everyone in the cozy bookstore looked up, momentarily distracted. He stepped back and crossed his arms, glaring at the wayward books. *Crap!* Before he could pick them up, he heard the distinctive CLACK-CLACK-CLACK-CLACK of chunky heels announcing the arrival of the preorder woman.

Leaving the jumble of books, he fished through the HOLD drawer. In the brown paper wrapper was the fourth, or maybe the fifth, title the woman had ordered by the same author. "Evelyn," he said, "I have your book right here." A warm, genuine smile complemented his friendly personality. Peering at her narrow glasses, he wondered how this single working mother could support herself and her newborn baby.

"Thank you for holding it for me," Evelyn said, one hand clutching the frayed lapel of her white cardigan. "I don't know what I'd do without romance books! They're my escape, my passion, my solace."

Kevin stared at her, his brown eyes blinking with curiosity through several seconds of silence. *Maybe you could find somebody to have a real relationship with,* he thought as he handed her the book. As if she read his thought, a hint of a smile played on her lips before she turned to leave. He and other covert eyes watched as she clumped back toward the door.

∗ ∗ ∗

Evelyn was too engrossed in her novel to notice the shouts and laughter of children playing around her. She liked to sit at the park's entrance across the beachfront high-rises on Flagler Street. Even as downtown fortunes declined, it still reminded her of when Bayfront Park was known for political gatherings and free musical performances by local bands.

After a particularly steamy scene, Evelyn took a break from her book and leaned over to plant a kiss on her son's forehead. The steady hum of traffic had lulled Herman to sleep, his face serene and delicate, like the cherubic babies on baby food jars. She always loved opening those jars, just to hear the pop of the lid. Herman rustled beneath the blanket, knocking his white chicken cap with its clever red felt wattle askew. Passersby often stopped and exclaimed over how unusual and adorable the hat was. Herman opened his mouth to cry, but sleep claimed him first. A yawn bloomed wide as a meteorite flake tumbled from the sky and vanished down his throat.

Infancy and early childhood are crucial stages in developing a healthy body. Cells divide and multiply rapidly, allowing a child to develop a complex brain that will enable survival. But when the celestial dust speck drifted into Herman's protein-rich saliva, it disrupted this delicate process. Possessing wound-healing and antibacterial properties, the protein histatin caused the nucleus of hydrogen and helium to dissociate and collapse. Raw proton matter entered the child's body, fusing with his DNA. The new parent cells multiplied rapidly, spreading into the farthest capillaries of his toes and fingers with the usual genetic instructions that normal human DNA would bear. However, the cells' new primary directive was to flourish and give abundant life, just as stars spring from dust and gases in the billions. In the chaos of transformation, Herman's DNA interpreted the unknown element as polyethylene, a synthetic echo of something it could not name.

Friday, October 28, 1966.

That was strange. Evelyn could have sworn she heard a word—an actual word—spoken from Herman's room. She rose from the couch and left her book on the armrest, marking her spot. She cracked the door to his room and peered inside. Herman had pushed up into a sphinx pose, head high and back arched, his knit ladybug cap made him irresistibly adorable.

"There you are, my little dumpling," Evelyn said. She picked him up and dandled him above her head. "Are you trying to speak?" Herman kicked his feet and giggled when Evelyn blew raspberries on his pudgy tummy. "Say it again. Come on," she cooed between raspberries. "Say, Mama."

Herman didn't answer except to lift one of his delicate eyebrows. His hand reached for her nose and patted her cheek. Evelyn laid him back in the crib and tucked the blanket around him. After kissing him gently on the forehead, she turned to leave when, unexpectedly, she heard the sound again.

"Maa-maa."

Evelyn looked over her shoulder, startled.

Funny, the voice seems to have come from that rubber doll.

Herman only smiled and squirmed. There was nothing unusual about the crib. Everything looked perfectly normal. Several stuffed animals sat with their backs against the vertical wooden slats. Among them, a vintage doll held both arms extended as if asking to be picked up.

Intrepidly, Evelyn picked up the doll and turned it

over. The mechanical "Maa-maa" wheezed out as air moved through the weighted crier. "Most peculiar," she said, setting the doll back in its spot and telling herself it had simply shifted. "Now you sit there and go to sleep," she scolded.

Evelyn kissed her son and wiped the lipstick from his forehead. "And you go to sleep as well." She shook an admonishing finger at him. Herman wriggled playfully, licking his bottom lip as a trail of saliva glistened down his chin. When Evelyn turned to leave, she heard the sound again.

"Mama."

A cold tingle ran down her spine. Her heart skipped a beat as she threw an uneasy glance over her shoulder. Her throat was dry, each breath scraping like sandpaper. Living alone was unraveling her nerves; a simple creak of a door or shutter crash was all it took.

Pull yourself together, Evelyn.

As she inched toward the crib, the wooden floor creaked beneath her. The doll sat innocently with its back against the bars. It had not fallen over, which would have explained the mechanical crier blurting out the word. A rush of adrenaline coursed through her.

Why couldn't you have fallen? Her eyes probed the doll, its arms outstretched, face blank, staring into nothing.

Then it turned its head toward her.

"Mama. Mama. Mama."

Evelyn shrieked and clapped a quivering hand to her mouth. Each contraction of her heart shot ice through her veins. Breath caught in her throat as if the air had been sucked out of the room. Still as ever, the doll sat with both arms eerily motionless, its unblinking eyes fixed on her as if anticipating her next move. It seemed to yearn for affection, but only silence greeted its silent plea. Then, to her shock, it rolled over, pushed onto all fours, and stood erect.

"Oh my gosh!" Evelyn's mouth hung open in disbelief. She felt faint but stood her ground, legs quaking and one hand wrapped around the crib rail for support.

The doll balanced on the mattress and took its first baby steps, its tiny feet making soft indentations on the bed.

"Stay away from us!" Evelyn cried out. She scooped her son up and stumbled across the room. Trembling, she tried to grasp the doorknob, but her fingers refused to respond. *Open the door, Evelyn!* Her thoughts screamed. *Think of your son's safety!*

Finally, her fingers gripped, twisted, and the door swung wide.

Daring a glance behind her, Evelyn saw the doll had already climbed the liftgate, one leg hooked over the top. She shrieked, slammed the door behind her, and bolted across the living room. Blindly, she retreated until her back struck the entrance. Her legs gave out, and she slid to the floor, weeping. As silence pressed in, she stared up at Herman's bedroom door, bracing for what lay beyond. But it stayed shut—its stillness somehow more terrifying than movement. *Will it climb up and twist the doorknob?* Her fingers trembled against Herman's back, clutching him tighter than she meant to. Whatever that thing was in her son's room, it couldn't get out. At least, she hoped.

Lulled by her fearful whimpers and gentle rocking, Herman slept. Before long, she nodded off, exhausted by the emotional trauma.

Several minutes later, Evelyn felt the soft patting of Herman's hand against her mascara-smeared cheek. The touch prickled her skin, but it wasn't enough to wake her from her nightmare. Images of rubber dolls twirled, their twisted smiles and razor-sharp teeth mocking her with unblinking eyes. They circled weightlessly, slapping her face with clammy hands, leaving scratches that bloomed across her skin. Each sting made her body twitch, fighting to awaken. A scream echoed in her mind.

Jolting awake, Evelyn cried out, confused and unsettled. It took her a moment to realize the patting on her face was her son, cooing contentedly and learning how to spit bubbles. His eyes momentarily comforted her, but her fears of walking dolls immediately resurfaced. She struggled to her feet and placed him on the sofa, where he nestled among a doll and a few plush animals she'd arranged like a soft barricade. Normally, she'd indulge in nonsense baby talk, but her thoughts remained tethered to the thing pacing his bedroom.

She crept toward Herman's room, pausing between steps to keep the floor from creaking and attracting the doll's attention. The anxiety came in waves. Heart beating, she held her breath and pressed her ear against the door. Complete silence. Evelyn reached out, her skin prickling as she turned the doorknob. When the hinge squeaked, her heart skipped a beat. But Evelyn, unfazed, poked her head in and peered through the crack.

The doll stood in the middle of the room, like a faithful dog waiting for its owner to come home. Extending both arms, it cried, "Mama, Mama, Mama."

Evelyn gasped and slammed the door shut, shaking the walls. She clutched her hair and cried, "Why is this happening?" Cupping her lips with a quivering hand, she turned back to her baby on the sofa. Herman was on his stomach, attempting to grab the doll that had fallen forward. He kicked his plump legs, inching closer. While he sucked on his fist, a chilling thought flashed through her mind.

"Herman, don't," she whispered.

His tiny hand reached for the doll, and a faint electrical spark pierced its rubber shoulder. For the first time, she witnessed her son give life to an inanimate object. Its vacant expression unchanged, the doll turned its head, moving left to right and then back again as if getting rid of any kinks. Evelyn froze and dared not breathe.

The doll opened its eyes and sat up, then looked at Herman and said, "Mama." Miraculously, it stood, holding its arms out for balance.

Seconds crawled by as Evelyn clutched the lapel of her cardigan, her eyes blinking in astonishment. The doll stroked Herman's smooth face, feeling his nose, warm skin, and fluttering lips as he burbled. It stared without expressing any emotion, blinking out of instinct rather than necessity. Herman kicked his curled toes in delight each time the doll spoke. It meant no harm. Evelyn's fear slowly unraveled, and a shaky giggle broke through her disbelief. She stepped forward, cautious and captivated, watching the two side by side on the sofa; one made of flesh and blood and the other of rubber.

Kneeling beside Herman, Evelyn studied the doll closely. Twelve inches tall, it wore a blank expression, no smile, no warmth, just wide blue eyes, faded rosy cheeks, and glossy pink lips. Soft brown eyebrows arched beneath wisps of synthetic blond hair. A striped collar lent charm to its short-sleeved yellow dress, and its pumpkin-colored socks, snug and fuzzy like a woolly bear caterpillar, peeked out from beneath fringed moccasins.

The doll approached Evelyn and touched her face. "Mama," it said, the voice mechanism sliding back into place with a soft metallic clink. Evelyn smiled excitedly.

Questions swarmed her mind, and the lack of answers terrified her. With a simple touch of his tiny fingers, Herman had transformed an inanimate toy into a living creature, defying logic. Then concern twisted her stomach. If her son's ability were exposed, the Department of Homeland Security or another shadowy government agency would surely take him away. A swarm of strangers in white hazmat suits would poke and prod him in the name of scientific research. She shuddered. *There's no way in hell I'll let anyone take my son away. I'll fight them to the death if I have to!*

Anxious to face the first doll, Evelyn approached her son's bedroom with trepidation. With a click, she unlatched the door and pushed it open. The doll was still standing patiently in the center. It looked up at her and blinked its eyes using the weighted eyelid lever. Its facial expression showed no emotion. "Mama," it cried, air sipping out of the mechanism. It stepped forward, then awkwardly ran toward her, managing to keep its balance. Evelyn's eyebrows shot up in astonishment, and a smile broke across her face. Stopping at her feet, the doll tilted its head upward and patted her shin. "Mama," it repeated. Evelyn marveled at the feel of its tiny rubber hand.

Ding dong!

The doorbell chime startled her.

Evelyn turned quickly, knocking the doll over. *Not a good time for Girl Scout cookies!* The doll was already rising when she grabbed it by the waist. She hurried to the sofa, where the other doll was playfully patting Herman's nose, and snatched it by the arm, making it squeak in protest.

The doorbell chimed again.

"Coming," Evelyn hollered, clutching the two dolls to her chest. She opened the closet door and flung the dolls inside, leaving the door ajar. Evelyn breathed a sigh of relief. After taking a moment to regain her composure, she answered the door.

"Ms. Sinclair?" The woman's nasal voice made Evelyn's skin crawl.

"Yes?"

"Are you okay?"

Evelyn stared at her blankly for a moment, then said, "Of course. Why do you ask?"

"I thought I heard someone crying, and I was worried something had happened," the neighbor said. She craned her neck to see inside, concern and curiosity competing in her eyes, but Evelyn sidestepped to block

14

her view. "You have a cute baby, Ms. Sinclair. But you shouldn't leave him unattended. He might fall off the couch and hurt himself."

"Thank you. That's very kind of you, Ms. . . . ?" Evelyn asked through gritted teeth.

"Olivia Sanders," she said, sniffing with interest. Her palpable eagerness gave Evelyn the creeps— curious people were likely to gossip and spread rumors. "My husband, Taylor, and I live in apartment ten, right next door. If you need anything, don't hesitate to call us."

Evelyn flashed a dismissive smile. "Thank you, Mrs. Sanders. I appreciate your concern, but I assure you, everything is fine here." A doll walked across the living room floor.

As the neighbor walked away, Evelyn noticed the empty drinking glass in her hand. *She must have been propping it against the wall to eavesdrop.* She closed the door and clicked the deadbolt into place. "That was close," she said, leaning against the door and clutching the lapel of her cardigan. Keeping the dolls a secret wouldn't be easy—not with a snoopy neighbor like Mrs. Sanders.

Tuesday, May 14, 1968.

Herman's lack of interest in speech and his refusal to make eye contact worried Evelyn. He had begun banging his head softly against the wall for reasons she couldn't explain. Every daycare turned them away after a single visit. It was the start of his isolation and a string of doctor's visits Evelyn hadn't expected.

"Those are cute bunny ears," the medical assistant said after taking Herman's temperature and making a note on the chart. Lily wrinkled her freckled nose and teased, "Let me see you hop like a bunny."

Herman clenched his fists and hopped across the room, not letting up. The soft chenille ears flopped vigorously.

"He has plenty of caps at home," Evelyn said, nodding. She took his hand and guided him onto the chair. Herman squirmed, slid off his chair, and continued bouncing, a smile back on his face. "I guess it's my fault."

Lily tilted her head, her pixie cut sharp and clean, drawing focus to her eyes and cheekbones. "What do you mean?"

"He's worn caps since he was a baby. I guess he got used to the feeling, and now he won't go without one."

"I see," she said, watching the child's antics. "And what happens when you take it off?"

"He throws a tantrum," said Evelyn with an embarrassed shrug.

"Well, we don't need a tantrum here, so please make sure those ears stay put," Lily said, winking as she closed the door behind her.

Several minutes later, there was a soft rap on the door. Dr. Lloyd entered the room, holding Herman's chart in one hand and closing the door with the other. His lab coat hung open, revealing a blue shirt and a gold tie with a diamond pattern. "Hello, Herman," he said, his perfectly straight teeth gleaming in a broad smile. "Where's your red crabby hat with the claws that you wore last week?" Evelyn thought his laugh sounded forced. "I was afraid you were going to try and pinch me again today!"

Herman didn't answer. His happy hopping twisted into an agitated thrash, his eyes darting everywhere except at Dr. Lloyd, who gave a slight nod, as if confirming what he already knew. "I'm curious, Ms. Sinclair, why is he wearing mittens?"

"My son scratches his face a lot," she said, surprised by how easily the lie slipped out. In truth, she didn't want her son to handle any toys in public, let alone give life to them. Securely tied shoelaces around the base of his mittens ensured that would never happen.

"Let's get you up on the exam table," Dr. Lloyd said, getting a hand under each arm. As soon as Herman's feet left the ground, his anger flared. He kicked and twisted, trying to get out of the doctor's firm grip. Even with the mittens, his hands latched onto the doctor's arm.

"Easy there, Herman," Dr. Lloyd said, his voice soothing. But Herman snapped, lunging at the doctor's arm with bared teeth. Dr. Lloyd winced but didn't loosen his grip. "It's okay, Herman," he said softly, stroking the boy's hair with his free hand. "I understand. We're going to help you feel better."

Herman's grip loosened, his anger fading into exhaustion. Taking this opportune moment, Dr. Lloyd put his large hands on the child's face for a quick look at his eyes. There were no epicanthic skin folds on the inner corners of his eyes, no white Brushfield spots on the iris, and no evidence of a flat nasal bridge. An inspection of his hands and feet failed to reveal a single transverse palmar crease or unusual spacing between the large and second toe.

"Open your mouth and stick your tongue out, like this," Dr. Lloyd said, demonstrating with a quick flick of his own tongue. Herman mimicked him, watching the wooden stick until his eyes crossed. No protruding or enlarged tongue evident, no ear problems noted, no heart, lung, or gastroesophageal concerns indicated.

His physical examination complete, Dr. Lloyd placed Herman on his mother's lap and leaned back in his rolling chair. "I've spoken with numerous other specialists since your last visit, and as a group, we failed to determine any concrete answer. However, Herman's blood tests have raised some disturbing questions.

"Ms. Sinclair," he said, scratching his head, his short, sandy hair springing back into place. "Is your son's crib made of metal?"

"No," she said, giving him a baffled look.

"Has he ever drunk any cleaning solution or detergent, anything stored under the kitchen sink?"

"Of course not!" *Just get to the point!*

Dr. Lloyd inclined his head, his expression composed. "Has he ever swallowed any coins?"

"Doctor, what is wrong with my son?" she asked flatly, her eyes pleading. The suspense was killing her. She fidgeted.

"I forwarded your son's blood sample to a specialty laboratory because my lab found traces of helium and hydrogen compounds. The presence of aluminum-26 and manganese-53 leads us to believe he swallowed a metallic object at some point." Dr. Lloyd shook his head. "I know it sounds incredible, but the composition of his blood is suggestive of meteorites."

Unable to comprehend the medical jargon, Evelyn bit her lower lip to keep it from quivering. She hesitated before asking, "Are you telling me my son has Down syndrome?"

"No," he said, closing the chart and tossing it on his desk. "I just examined him for traits of the condition, and he is physically fine. Down syndrome is a cell division disorder resulting in an extra chromosome 21, or trisomy 21, and prior tests have given no evidence of a chromosomal disorder. Your standard prenatal screening didn't reveal any indicators of the condition."

She nodded, still confused. "What about autism?"

His eyes narrowed, lost in thought. "Does he stack things obsessively, or consistently put his toys in a straight line?"

She shook her head.

"We do know the presence of abnormal compounds in cells can inhibit the body's absorption of iodine and other essential minerals, which are crucial for synthesizing hormones like thyroxine and triiodothyronine," he said, though he knew the words meant nothing to her. "Iodine deficiency results in the deceleration of physical and mental development. In your son's case, a significant deficiency appears to be impacting his mood, behavior, and overall growth."

"What will happen to him?" she asked, holding Herman closer.

Dr. Lloyd wished he could answer her question, but he didn't have a clue. Despite years of medical training, he had never encountered, let alone heard of, a case like Herman's. He and his associates had spent hours debating and theorizing only to reach an impasse and conclude that this child should not be alive.

"This disease is new to the medical field," Dr. Lloyd said without averting his gaze. "But it's already been labeled as Hydrolium syndrome, HHe syndrome, or 1-2 syndrome, for the atomic numbers of hydrogen and helium." He leaned forward, his eyes compassionate.

"Without those minerals, his moods may be volatile. He may appear timid one moment and experience bouts of rage the next, posing a risk to himself and others," he said, shrugging. "Herman's social skills may be limited and destructive."

Dr. Lloyd reached for his chrome-plated pen and scribbled on a notepad. "With your permission, we would like to conduct more tests. I'm giving you a referral to Dr. . . . ."

"No," Evelyn said, her voice firm despite the tremor underneath. She slipped on her sunglasses, shielding her puffy eyes, then swept her child into the crook of her arm and left the room.

"Ms. Sinclair?" The doctor stared after her, perplexed.

Evelyn broke down in tears as she stepped out of the medical building. She squeezed her son as she wept silently, ignoring the strange stares from people as they walked around her.

Herman put his arms around her neck and patted her back.

Friday, July 3, 1970.

At four years old, Herman's favorite activity was spending the day at Bayfront Park. Already dressed in his play clothes, he sat patiently while his mother retrieved his sneakers from the balcony, where they'd been left out to dry. Everywhere she went, the dolls followed her like puppies starved for affection. They often collided with her legs, rising only to extend their little arms and say, "Mama." While her son demanded most of her time and attention, Evelyn also had to constantly keep track of the dolls. They were almost as difficult to manage as Herman. She grabbed her romance novel from the kitchen counter and slipped it into the tote bag. After one final sweep of the apartment, she strapped Herman in his stroller and bustled out the door, hoping the sun wouldn't be too hot this early.

As soon as she left, the two dolls roamed freely, banging into furniture and occasionally knocking things over. One noticed that the balcony glass door was slightly ajar and pushed it open . . .

On the other side of the wall, Gregory sat on his bed listening to what sounded like the faint pattering of footsteps next door. *They sound . . . mechanical?* If he listened carefully, he could pick up a word or two. He flung the comic book aside, jumped out of bed, and placed his ear against the cool surface of the wall. His mother, Olivia, had told him that a real detective uses all five senses. "Look and listen to the faintest detail, and you shall become as good as they are," she had encouraged, knowing her son had set his heart on becoming a detective, which was evident by his passion for cop shows.

No one was home at Ms. Sinclair's apartment, that much he felt sure of. He had seen her striding past the window with her son in the stroller. This was his first clue that something wasn't right.

Gregory grabbed his plastic gun and shoved it into his back pocket. He slid the balcony door open and crept along the outside wall. The pulsing theme song to the Hawaiian cop show played in his head as he pulled the gun out and held it close to his shoulder. Standing barefoot, Gregory inched his way toward the edge of the balcony. He could hear faint patting sounds coming from the other side. *A burglar! Now it's up to me to catch the thief red-handed.* He peered around the wall and quickly pulled back to consider his next move. The element of surprise was crucial in apprehending suspects. Quietly, he clambered onto the wrought iron railing, balancing precariously with his free hand on the wall. This was it. The moment he'd trained for in his living room for years. He closed his eyes, counted to three, and leaned around the corner with his gun aimed.

"Stop, or I'll shoot!"

Gregory wavered in shock.

Two dolls were bent over, patting a cat figurine next to a flowerpot, their nylon hair waving in the soft breeze. Then they saw him—or at least, their eyes seemed to track him, though he was certain they couldn't see. They stood, arms raised. "Mama," they cried in unison as they stepped forward, their lips eerily still. A tremor shot through Gregory, knocking loose his grip on the wall. His fingers scraped past the railing—then he was falling. His last mental image was the balcony shrinking above him before he hit the floor.

Tuesday, July 21, 1970. 11:20 a.m.

Gregory thought he was awake. He swore his eyes were open and moving, but nothing registered, just darkness. "Moms," he said in alarm, his bandaged head shaking side to side. "Where are you?"

"I'm right here, Son," Olivia said, holding his hand, though she knew it offered little comfort.

"I can't see you!" Gregory thrashed in the narrow bed.

"Try to stay calm," she told him soothingly as she held him down. "You had a nasty fall, and now you're in the hospital. The doctor said you're going to be fine. You have a concussion that has temporarily affected your sight, but it will return in a few days." A lie. After three weeks at his side, shedding endless tears over his coma, Olivia was thrilled to see her son awake. The doctor had warned her that with such severe head trauma, Gregory might never regain his sight. It depended on whether the swelling around the cerebral cortex subsided quickly enough to avoid permanent damage.

"Moms, I don't want to be blind," Gregory cried, clutching the sheets as his heart raced. "I can't be a good cop if I'm blind."

"When you grow up, you will be a great detective," she said, kissing him gently.

Gregory stopped flailing, his breath ragged. He saw himself falling as the railing slipped farther away. And then there were the dolls. Blank-eyed, heads tilted in curiosity. Reaching with stiff, deliberate arms and calling to him in their mechanical voices. "Moms, I saw two dolls walking around on Ms. Sinclair's balcony! They're alive! They talked to me!"

"Gregory," she said with a slight frown. "You hit your head hard. Let's concentrate on healing so you can regain your eyesight."

"Moms, I'm telling you the truth! I *did* see two walking dolls. Ms. Sinclair is keeping a secret in her apartment. If you don't believe me, go over and see for yourself!"

Believing every word he said, Olivia held his hand in hers. She remembered her encounter with Evelyn as if it had happened yesterday. Since then, she'd heard strange noises and wondered about the odd, secretive woman next door. *Whatever she's hiding, I'll expose her. She'll pay for what she's done to Gregory, no matter how long it takes!*

After a long week, Gregory regained his sight and was released from the hospital.

Monday, September 8, 1980. 6:17 p.m.

Now fourteen, Herman bounced arrhythmically, snapping his fingers to the fast robotic beat of his favorite new-wave song. Perched atop his head, the cow hat spun as he whipped and stomped. For a moment, the cow seemed alive, grinning wide, tongue lolling, its tiny bell jingling like it too was partying hard.

Evelyn clutched her sides, gasping for breath between fits of laughter. Every time she saw the ridiculous cap, the giggles spilled out. And though she'd never admit it, the contagious tune had wormed its way into her heart too.

Herman stopped dancing momentarily and crossed his eyes to focus on the bell above his forehead. He shook his head. *Ting-a-ling-a-ling!* Laughing, he repeated the action several more times. If the record hadn't ended, he might have kept at it all day.

"What do you want to hear now, Mr. Cow?" Evelyn asked, still laughing as she picked up the vinyl.

He didn't have to think twice. "You Must Snap It!"

"But we just played it a thousand times. Are you sure you want to hear it again?"

Herman's smile faded.

"You Must Snap It!" he screamed, slapping her face.

Evelyn staggered back, her cheek stinging from the unexpected slap. Her eyes watered as she fought the wave of hurt.

* * *

Miami-Sunset Area. Wednesday, January 15, 1964.

Visiting Nautical South Mall was always a treat for Evelyn. Over the years, she watched the mall transform into a unique shopping experience. With a vision to make Nautical South a water wonderland, the developer installed a series of aquariums along every pathway, each meticulously designed to showcase different marine life. Shoppers marveled at the enchanting atmosphere of colorful fish and intricate coral reefs as they strolled from store to store.

Nautical South was where Evelyn had met Berto García-Famosa, a recent Cuban emigrant. She fell hard and quick. His laughter curled around her like a warm blanket. And when he leaned in, eyes glinting over his sexy low voice, her pulse stuttered. Even the language barrier felt like flirtation. Weeks later, at his home, Evelyn discovered he despised the English version of his name. He would playfully slam his fist on the kitchen counter and say, "Mi nombre es Berto, not Bert!" She would ruffle his curly hair to further annoy him and softly whisper, "Bert."

Several months later, against her parents' wishes, they were married. The months that followed were marked by quiet joy, anticipation, and a growing sense of family. Then, everything unraveled. In March 1966, just months before the birth of their baby, Berto was an innocent bystander shot in a drug-related shoot-out and lost his life. Evelyn's world was shattered—at just twenty-nine, she struggled to navigate the over-whelming emotional challenges of being a grieving widow. For years, she couldn't bear to hear her husband's name spoken aloud, let alone carry it as her own. Quietly, Evelyn reverted to her birth name. Despite her adversities, she managed to sustain herself and her baby with her husband's life insurance policy, which she later invested in Miami's booming economy.

Nautical South Mall. Tuesday, September 16, 1980.

Evelyn browsed through the blouses, hangers scraping against the metal rack. She could never resist a 15 percent discount at her favorite store, despite the risks of taking Herman out. *A little bit of sun and fresh air will do him good*, she convinced herself. Herman—sporting a jester's cap made of purple, gold, and green felt, adorned with bells—stood by her side. The gold bells tinkled whenever he shifted his head vigorously.

Evelyn tapped her son on the shoulder. "Honey, Mommy is going to try on these two blouses," she said, lifting his chin and forcing him to look into her eyes.

"Promise me you'll stay right here and not get into trouble."

"I promise," he said, wiggling and nodding so the bells chimed.

With Evelyn out of sight, Herman began jumping to make the bells jingle louder, giggling and flailing his arms. Shoppers turned and stared, snickering as his movements grew more manic. "I'm a joker," he said, slapping the bell with his covered hand. He hopped into the next aisle like a giant bunny, making the bells ring in unison. "I'm a joker," he sang.

"You mean a jester," a girl with long auburn hair and green eyes corrected him. She gazed at his tricolored hat with scorn. "Why are you wearing that stupid hat?"

"My jester hat is beautiful," he said, a frown creasing his forehead.

"Well, I guess the colors are pretty, but I wouldn't be caught dead in it," she said haughtily. She slapped the nearest bell. Forgetting his annoyance, Herman reached up and hit the same bell, but the chime sounded muffled.

"No, not like that," the girl exclaimed, rolling her eyes. "It'll ring better if you remove the stupid gloves."

She grabbed his hand and tugged at the knot. The first one came off so easily, she attacked the second one and threw them both on the floor as if they were dirty socks. "Now you can hit it better," she said triumphantly, folding her arms across her chest and stepping back.

Herman batted at the tiny bell with his bare hand; the sound rang out clearly. He jumped in a circle, laughing and singing, celebrating his accomplishment. Turning back to give the girl another chance, he realized she had vanished.

Evelyn returned the fitting room tags to the clerk and hurried back to where she'd left her son.

Her stomach dropped. He was gone.

The blouses slipped from her trembling hands and tumbled to the floor.

"Herman!" she cried, her voice slicing through the store.

The overhead lights buzzed dimly as she wove through the aisles, mind spiraling with worst-case scenarios. Tears blurred her vision. Her heart thudded like a warning drum.

What if he left the store?

She froze. Her breath caught at the final thought.

I must find him before something horrible happens!

Panting, she darted down the main aisle, scanning each corridor. "Herman!" she shouted, oblivious to the stares. She veered sharply, nearly knocking a woman aside. "I'm sorry," she sobbed, barely slowing.

Fighting back tears, Evelyn worked her way toward the exit, where a woman stood examining the price tag of a sequined evening dress. Seizing the woman's arm, she asked, "Did you see a teenage boy in a jester cap go out?"

"I can't say that I have." The woman shook her head and patted Evelyn's shoulder. "If I see him, I'll tell him you're looking for him."

Evelyn offered a quick nod, eyes glossy with panic. "Thank you," she whispered, already half turned. She ran toward the men's department. *Maybe he followed someone over there!* Turning the corner, she caught sight of a clerk assisting a man wearing a short-brimmed hat, his right foot squeezing into a tasseled loafer.

"Pardon me," said Evelyn, her chest heaving. Her swollen eyes—twin bruises of anguish—met theirs. "Did you see a teenage boy wearing a silly cap?" She clung to hope.

The clerk, seemingly indifferent to Evelyn's plight, shook his head and returned his attention to the man wearing the hat.

Suddenly, a familiar voice chimed from the men's suit department.

"Beautiful people."

"Herman?" Her heart skipped.

Without thinking, Evelyn bolted, her heart overflowing with joy. Her fondest memory of Herman was his contagious, heartfelt laughter. It was therapeutic. Good for the mind and soul. But most importantly, it was genuine. She couldn't imagine sitting at the kitchen table over coffee without it.

The unmistakable jester's hat popped into view, and Evelyn's heart surged. Blood pounded in her ears as she pushed forward, desperate to reach her son before anything could go wrong. But then she saw it, her worst fear unfolding. Her jaw dropped, eyes wide and brimming with panic.

"Don't touch it!" she cried, reaching out.

Herman stood inches from a suited mannequin, his finger slowly extending toward its plastic hand. A flicker passed from fingertip to fingertip, a life-giving spark.

Time fractured.

The mannequin turned its head toward Herman, joints unfolding like a bear waking from a long winter's nap. Unlike the rubber dolls at home, this figure underwent a refined transformation. Its fiberglass shell served as a perfect conduit for a neurological link with Herman. The eerie figure tried to move but faltered, restrained by metal brackets clamped around its legs. It tilted its head, vacant eyes fixed on the bind. Radiation from the foreign elements coursing through its frame softened the fiberglass until the leg oozed through the clamp. Then, stepping from the riser, it collapsed with a resounding clatter, limbs splayed in a most unnatural sprawl.

The floor manager ran to the scene, where she noticed the mannequin lying face down on the floor as if it had been clobbered with a blunt object. A teenage boy stood beside it, his eyes sparkling with delight. She had caught him red-handed. *These young punks will do anything for attention these days*, she thought.

Annoyance etched across her face, the manager threw Evelyn a look. "Lady, is *he* with you?"

Evelyn remained in shock, her vacant eyes drifting toward the mannequin on the floor.

With a stern expression, the manager turned to Herman and took a firm hold of his elbow. "This is not funny, young man. I want you to—"

A tapping sound interrupted her tirade. She looked down and blinked in disbelief as the mannequin's white hand slapped at the floor several times, as though searching for something. She gasped and released the boy. The thing put both hands on the floor and pushed, lifting its upper torso. Then it lifted its gaze like a predator, taking in its surroundings and calculating its next move.

Holding the lapel of her cardigan and shaking her head, Evelyn stared as though witnessing the resurrection of Lazarus. Herman was dancing and grunting, elated by his creation. Meanwhile, the manager stood frozen, unable to scream. Even if she could, no one would be foolish enough to help. Her mouth opened, but no words flowed. Only shallow, panicked gasps escaped.

As the mannequin lifted itself from the floor, the manager's eyes filled with panic. Her head jerked. *This can't be happening*, she thought, grabbing at her heart before she collapsed. Evelyn wanted to help, but she was too frightened to react.

Then it stood.

On its own.

And took a single step.

On its own.

Unless the shoppers were paying close attention, none could detect the low frequency emitted by the polyethylene figure. The sound encased visual, emotional, and episodic impressions—details like time of day, spatial context, and the mannequin's presence— in a fragile bubble before they could settle into long-term memory. Every human who witnessed the figure was affected, as if by a disease. Only Evelyn and her son remained immune, bound by the shared DNA that linked them to the creature.

"Come here," Evelyn cried out. Unsure of the mannequin's capabilities, she insisted, "Come *here,* Herman!"

Content with his new friend, the boy hopped about excitedly, but he failed to understand that friends are made of flesh and blood.

The mannequin flaunted a navy pin-striped suit with a white button-down and a bold tie, exuding the image of a top business professional at a prestigious firm. Black leather shoes set off the patterned pima cotton socks. A handsome fellow with a square chin and robust lips, CEO turned its milky-white head, its face unchanging. It didn't smile. It didn't breathe. It didn't even blink its glassy, unseeing eyes. They were fixed in an eternal stare that betrayed no soul, only the illusion of presence. CEO took slow, awkward steps that mimicked the walking dead. Unlike the rotting corpses on the silver screen, the eerie creature became skilled at walking with each careful movement.

The spark that brought the mannequin to life triggered a chain reaction in the fiberglass body. Daughter cells divided into trillions through mitosis, each nucleus encoded with DNA instructions that urged the host to search for and give life to others. It yearned to multiply and preserve its species as any life on earth.

As its sense of purpose solidified, the creature sprinted down the aisles with unwavering resolve, its vacant gaze sweeping through the store and its footsteps hammering the ceramic tiles.

The man in the brimmed hat was next to encounter the mannequin's chilling movements. His eyes bulged and his mouth dropped open. "Holy mackerel!" he said as dread wrapped him like a cloak. Without thinking, he flung the bag with his new shoes at the anomaly before bolting.

As rumors of the possessed mannequin spread,

panic broke out. The looks of wonder were unlike any other in Miami's history, and it spread like the black plague. CEO created an uncanny valley[1], a dip in human response triggering revulsion. Shoppers recoiled in disgust as the business professional ran by in designer shoes. Children sought shelter behind their petrified parents, while others sought refuge among the endless clothing racks. Evelyn watched the dummy as it headed toward the boy's department.

Betraying no emotions, the unearthly figure stopped beside a rugged-looking mannequin in plaid flannel, jeans, and boots. Satisfied with its first find, CEO reached out and touched the mannequin's hand, sparking life into the figure just like Herman.

Evelyn flinched. Her eyes widened like a full moon rising. As she wove between the home décor displays, the sweet fragrance of lavender-scented candles clashed with the chaos unfolding before her. "Oh my," she murmured, stepping back in disbelief. Her hair clung to her face, damp and disheveled from running. *This is unbelievable! Only Herman can give life!*

This was precisely what she had always feared. To

---

[1] Masahiro Mori (1927-2025), "The Uncanny Valley," Energy 7, no. 4 (1970): 33-35.

protect the world from calamity, Evelyn had spent fourteen years cloistered, veiling Herman's hands on their rare, necessary excursions. But deep in her heart, she'd always known this day would eventually arrive.

Suddenly, Woody, the lumberjack, moved its head. On its own.

And like its predecessor, the burly figure emitted a low frequency that penetrated the minds of everyone who saw its creation. With uncanny focus, it carefully assessed the situation before acting. Heat from the elements softened the tissue around its fiberglass legs, allowing the dummy to detach from the metal stand with ease. Woody paused, aware that its purpose was to give life to others. It followed its genetic code flawlessly.

"What the hell is happening? Now there are two of them! Run!" a voice shouted.

Parents, pastors, police, and community leaders from every corner could hardly believe their eyes. The gap in the uncanny valley widened to Grand Canyon proportions. Shoppers backed away, unable to tear their eyes from it.

After witnessing the two mannequins sprint across the store, a woman dropped to her knees, clasped her hands together, and recited the Rosary in Spanish.

Woody veered down the aisle toward the praying woman, its rugged boots clomping against the tile floor, its molded face stern, hawklike brow unflinching.

Someone screamed, "Look out! It's coming this way!" The crowd scattered in sudden panic, and waves of screams splashed through the store as the sprinter clipped the praying woman, knocking her flat on her back.

Despite the turmoil, the duo continued to spark life in others, leading each creation to awaken and release a subtle frequency. Before terrified onlookers, Woody animated a mannequin that pulsed with a strange, magnetic coolness. The black-and-white checkered cap and scarf were nods to its nostalgic tastes. Its layered T-shirt and stonewashed jeans spoke of its laid-back, creative personality, hinting at sketching in a cozy café or exploring urban landscapes with a camera.

Like the others, Pixel sprang to life—its fixed eyes chilling, its limbs flailing with eerie urgency. It sprinted off, price tags snapping like panicked flags. Off balance, it collided with an older man, sending him hurtling into a belt rack with bone-jarring force. Metal clattered and leather tangled as the rack toppled, slicing open a deep gash above the man's left eyebrow.

Not one word of apology.

Pixel didn't even slow down.

A clearance sticker peeled off its elbow mid-run and landed on the man's chest like a ceremonial stamp.

Within minutes, life flourished like a weed patch after a heavy downpour. The seeds of life had been sown, and soon, the mannequins multiplied: two, then four, then eight, then sixteen. Some jogged and others ran, and though they all advanced independently, they somehow seemed to move as one. Hordes of shoppers dashed for the exits, screaming dire warnings as they scattered. Some fled before witnessing the terror.

Pixel stopped before a headless figure that gave the impression of a young marketing executive with a sharp eye for detail and color. Its fashion suggested a taste for art gallery openings and hidden city gems. The striped sweater added a touch of sophistication, while the sleek black suede jacket lent an edge of modernity. The clothes hummed with energy as Michelangelo animated, withdrawing its hands from the jacket's pockets and striding forward.

The headless figure stepped into the limelight like a solitary lantern in the woods, seeking the flickering spirits of forgotten mannequins, intent on igniting their stillness with the warmth of its spark. It shot across the floor and easily navigated the escalator's moving grates, the metallic hum mingling with the chatter of shocked shoppers. Disregarding the safety rail, Michelangelo swayed slightly during the descent. The scent of perfume wafted through the air, mixing with the faint aroma of freshly brewed coffee from a nearby café. Upon reaching the lower level, the creature was captivated by the mannequins in the women's department, each in a stylized pose and adorned in the latest fashion under bright, inviting lights.

Shopping for a suit to impress her boss, Grace heard the clatter of heavy shoes on the escalator, but was engrossed in the mauve two-piece suit to notice the headless dummy. She held the suit up to see how it looked in the mirror, admiring how it draped the contours of her body and trying to decide if it was in her color set. Her gaze traveled along the neatly pressed slacks. Then, out of the corner of her eye, she caught sight of the brown shoes and black trousers of someone behind her. The stranger stood uncomfortably close, practically breathing down her neck without the decency of an "Excuse me." Uneasy, she turned sharply and said in a sarcastic tone, "May I help y—"

Her knees buckled, and her head snapped back, way back. A jumble of shock and fear left her paralyzed, and then she let out an ear-piercing scream, her uvula visibly vibrating at the back of her throat. Grace was sure the devil himself had come to drag her into the bowels of hell, punishment for the years she'd spent quietly embezzling from the firm. She dropped the suit and swung her tiger-print tote bag at the dummy as if swatting an elusive fly.

Michelangelo jerked painlessly at each blow, but it was learning quickly and formulating its next move. A deft thrust of its hand yanked the purse from her grasp, and in the same movement raked it at her head, leaving a row of crimson welts across her forehead. Still screaming, Grace shielded her head with her delicate hands. One final blow struck her hard across the jaw with a wicked uppercut that snapped her head back and sent her sprawling, unconscious, onto the now-rumpled suit. Her flailing fingers caught the purse strap, pulling Michelangelo down on top of her.

Terrified women stood frozen, their eyes locked on the nightmarish scene. They watched from a safe distance, too petrified to intervene. Someone in the crowd mistook it for a sci-fi film shoot. But when he realized there were no cameras and no famous movie stars, his face was a portrait of fear.

One woman decided she'd seen enough. Determined, she launched herself at the mannequin as it struggled with the purse. She landed a flurry of blows on its shoulders, her floral dress fluttering. The crowd watched in stunned silence. Two other women, thinking there was safety in numbers, joined the assault. They kicked and beat the effigy, their faces contorting with fierce pleasure.

Then, as the creature rose, the blows ceased.

A dreadful silence fell over the aisle as the women quailed at the sight. Their impulse to assist the unconscious woman now seemed ill-advised. Paralyzed by fear, they cowered in the face of such an inexorable force. Not a single word escaped their trembling lips. Michelangelo twisted and slung the tiger-print tote. Its momentum carved a brutal path across the women's faces, dropping the first like a broken doll. The other two abandoned the fight before the mannequin could unleash additional blows.

Now free to offer life, Michelangelo turned stiffly, trampling Grace underfoot as it resumed its mission.

At the far end of the aisle, a striking display featured five female mannequins in sequined evening gowns, each posed with stylized grace. Their presence demanded attention. Though their faces lacked human detail, they shimmered beneath the floodlights, their glossy surfaces frozen in ceremonial stillness like polished stone.

Elevated on a platform above the others, Crimson Elegance dominated the scene, cloaked in a floor-length scarlet gown with a plunging neckline. With arms outstretched in a fluid arc, it gave the illusion of motion, suspended mid-dance.

Michelangelo yearned to touch them. Raising its arm, the creature leaned forward and gently brushed its cold fingers over each one. As its fingertip brushed the fiberglass, a faint spark of energy flashed between them. Then, drawn by an unspoken call, the female mannequins tilted their polished heads in eerie unison, surveying the aisle with blank intention. They flexed their arms and legs to loosen the stiffness of their dormant state. Heat from the elements allowed their legs to ooze through the metal stands. Once free, they moved cautiously, their steps as tentative as a newborn fawn's until they mastered the fundamentals of balance

46

and propulsion.

Pandemonium overtook the store. Patrons scattered, yelping in fright as dread thickened behind the mannequins' procession. Led by Crimson Elegance, the newly awakened surged forward, searching for others like them, yearning to give life. Once every mannequin had stirred, they spilled into the mall and city streets, chaos trailing in their wake.

* * *

Cynthia's bushy eyebrows accentuated the warmth of her chestnut eyes, which her husband often admired. Her voluminous hair and double hoop earrings swayed as she turned to watch the fleeing crowd.

"What is happening? Why is everybody running?" she asked.

With concern etched across his face, Michael grabbed his pregnant wife by the elbow and pulled her back. "I don't know what's going on, but we'd better leave just the same."

Cynthia's pink lips parted in shock when she saw the first wave of animated mannequins. "Oh my," she said, her hand flying to her mouth. A drove of expressionless mannequins in a range of skin tones was streaming out of a large department store: some with heads, some without, and in a startling array of fashions, all running autonomously. She blinked at a sight that defied all reason.

"Let's go, Cynthia." Michael grabbed her arm, alarm tightening his voice.

"I can't run in my condition, Michael," she said, cradling her belly.

Michael scanned the area. Spotting a Japanese gift shop, he said, "Come on. We'll be safe here." Without hesitation, he pulled her inside and closed the glass door behind them.

The store was empty, except for the manager, Steven, and his assistant, Christian. Wearing a blue vest emblazoned with the store's logo, Steven hollered from behind the counter, "What do you think you're doing?"

"I'm saving our asses!" Michael said over his shoulder, not taking his weight off the door.

"Dude, you better leave before I call mall security." Steven clenched his fists as he confronted the young man, who refused to back down.

"Hey, guys! Check out the commotion out there!" All eyes turned toward Christian, whose rugged features and muscular build gave him the air of a seasoned boxer. "Like, that's totally freaky, man," he said.

Steven approached the glass door and stared as chaos flooded the mall corridor. Grim-faced, he reached into his pant pocket, withdrew a key, and locked the door with a decisive click.

"What the hell is going on?" he murmured. He flinched as a woman fell forward, spilling the contents of her purse. She rose quickly, slightly dazed from the fall, and continued running without retrieving her belongings.

The store manager grabbed Michael's shoulder. "Why is everyone running?" he shouted.

Michael looked at him, unsure how to answer. Before he could utter a word, they heard a thud against the glass door, making everyone flinch. Cynthia instantly panicked.

CEO loomed, plastered against the pane, its white, chalky face peering through the glass.

Cynthia sank to the floor, shaking her head at the vile thing while her husband and the two store clerks stood in awe. No one said a word. Michael backed up and knelt beside his wife, his eyes locked on the anomaly.

CEO leaned to one side for a better view of the store.

"It's looking for something," Steven said, voice low with unease.

Christian put his hands in his jacket and moved to block the dummy's view. The mannequin responded by leaning in the opposite direction, focusing on something behind the young man.

Michael stood sharply and pulled free of Cynthia's grasp, his eyes taking swift inventory of the store. The souvenir shop specialized in handmade Japanese crafts, including knives and fans, antique coins, and a variety of ninja darts. A display of beautifully crafted swords hung on the walls, but none stood out like the mannequin in full samurai regalia. It held a polished sword over its shoulder, poised to strike.

Christian gasped when he made the connection. "Are you thinkin' what I'm thinkin'?"

The glass door rattled.

Cynthia cried out in despair.

CEO struck the glass with its pale hands, then backed up and bashed into the door. It rattled on its hinges but held.

Cynthia covered her ears and shook her head. "Make it stop! Make it stop!" she screamed, rocking back and forth like a helpless child. "Just let it in and give it what it wants!"

Steven crouched in front of her. "Listen," he said, forcing her to look at him. "There's nothing we can do! Do you hear me? We don't know what that thing is, and I'm sure as hell not gonna let *it* in so we can have coffee and cake!"

"No shit, Sherlock." Michael pried Steven away from his wife. "The least we can do is push *that* counter against the door!"

Surging with adrenaline, Steven seized on the idea. *He's right. If we work together, we can haul the counter against the door to stop the mannequin from gaining entry.* The fire left his eyes as he nodded, ready to leap into action.

Christian grabbed one end of the counter and heaved, his curly hair bobbing as his muscles strained. Before they could swing the counter, the dummy slammed into the door, launching Cynthia into another fit of hysteria.

CEO backed up several feet, then surged forward, crashing through the door and scattering shards of glass. Steven and Michael immediately tackled the mannequin when it hit the floor. They punched and jabbed relentlessly, but there was no resistance. No cry for help. No surrender. Instead, CEO inched toward the samurai, pulling the two men along with it. Steven jammed his elbow into the dummy's spine, punishment no ordinary man could withstand. And yet, CEO crawled forward, undeterred.

"Out of the way!" Christian shouted feverishly.

Michael and Steven looked up just as Christian swung a Japanese sword overhead. The blade swooshed through the air as the two men scrambled off the intruder. Christian plunged the single-edged sword into the mannequin's neck, severing its head with a single, brutal stroke. He struck the creature several times with fierce determination, cursing with each slice into its synthetic body, shredding the expensive suit. The katana, now streaked with grime and synthetic fibers, quivered in his hands. Body parts wriggled briefly before going still.

Christian's face twisted in anger, sweat drenching his body. "Your mama! You hear me?" He pointed the sword at the mangled mannequin and repeated, "Your mama!"

"You need to take a chill pill, man. Can't you see he's already dead?" Steven said as he pushed him back.

"Your mama!" Christian had to get the last word in, his hand trembling from adrenaline. He spat at the dummy and shouted, "¡No juegues conmigo, puto!"

* * *

Westwood Lakes, seven miles northwest of Nautical South Mall.

Hunting lodge relics adorned the dark wood paneling of an outdoor supply store. Among them, a massive moose head with a 48" spread, a deer with an impressive eight-point rack, and numerous vintage rifles and handguns from the turn of the century. Behind the busts, a towering mural of a hunter aiming at a charging moose cemented the store's identity. The sharp scent of cedar, leather, and pine filled the air as framed photographs lined the south wall. Each captured a frozen thrill: past hunts, shared stories, and camaraderie. They turned the shop into more than a storefront. This was a gathering place, an altar to the outdoor life.

Frank Irving, who preferred to hunt deer in Jackson County, Florida, stood behind the old wooden counter proudly demonstrating his favorite big-game rifle.

"This is my most popular firearm, a standard bolt-action rifle available at a reasonable price. It's the kind of rifle serious hunters go for: clean design, dependable build, and real presence."

The client glanced at his wife, nodding his stamp of approval. After a stealthy look at the price tag, he said, "I'd expect it to be more expensive."

"The rifle has an aluminum floor plate, instead of steel. Aluminum alloy is lighter and less expensive. Plus, this model lacks the adjustable trigger on pricier models. I can give you an exceptional deal if you purchase the scope, bipod, and cartridge today."

What the fucking hell was that?!

He saw it out of the corner of his eye.

It was unusual for a mannequin to jog into the shop, especially one with its head thrown back and mouth wide in laughter. Blonde twin ponytails bobbed above slender shoulders as thin arms swung in stiff, robotic arcs. Tiny feet pumped with relentless energy, mimicking a thorough workout.

Frank jumped back, his salt-and-pepper eyebrows lifting. The two customers followed his gaze, and their mouths fell open in unison.

Gliding with unnatural grace, the artificial woman power-walked through an array of rods, reels, and tackle boxes, eyes locked on the lone male mannequin perched on a white riser, decked out in camouflage and gear. It lifted a finger and tapped the other as if playing a children's game of tag: You're it! No tag backs! A simple flick of its tiny finger was the only requirement. Then the creature jogged out with mincing steps and that silly laugh plastered on its face.

"I think we'd better go now," the customer said with a tremor in his voice. He grabbed his wife's arm. "We'll come back when you're not so busy."

Long frozen in a crouched position, peering through the scope of a rifle, the hunter moved its egg-shaped head. Beneath the pulled-up hood, there were no eyes or mouth, just dents where eyes should be and a slight mound for a nose. With mechanical focus, the figure surveyed the area, registering the rifle. Its gaze landed first on the wall-mounted moose, then drifted to the big game mural, a sprawl of sunbaked colors and wilderness shadows. The mural evoked a legacy the dummy seemed born to reenact. Then the connection formed: the camouflaged man, the rifle, the antlered moose. It was learning.

Still in hunting pose, the mannequin aimed at the North American bull mount and fired a single shot. No loud bang. No recoil. The mounted beast remained still without even flicking an ear. Mystified, Hunter tilted its head and hurled the weapon to the floor.

The proprietor and his two customers stood frozen as they watched the mannequin shift its legs, separating from the metal bracket that held it in place. It stood clumsily, teetered, then tumbled off the riser, crashing to the floor with a loud, hollow thump. Fumbling, it brought both legs in and pushed to its knees. Slowly, the creature placed one foot on the floor and stood precariously.

"Oh, my goodness," the woman cried, her knees buckling under her weight.

Hunter suddenly lunged forward like a child learning to walk. It knocked over several boots from a shelf, momentarily hindering its advance. But once it grasped the mechanics of balance, it surged forward.

The husband was the first to sprint across the floor, followed closely by his screeching wife. Frank Irving was left to face the unnatural being. In his adult life, he had faced charging bears and moose with antlers as wide as five feet without so much as a shiver. Today, he was afraid for the first time.

He snatched up the box of cartridges and ripped it open, scattering the bullets across the counter. With a trembling hand, he loaded a single bullet, slammed the bolt shut, and cocked the rifle with a sharp metallic snap. Before he could raise it, the unnerving figure stood before him and gripped the barrel with both hands, attempting to wrestle the firearm away. Its strength was unexpected, but Frank held on grimly through the bizarre tug of war. With one hand on the rifle, he struck the mannequin on its bulbous nose with the other. The creature staggered back, still holding the rifle.

No surprise registered on its blank face, but it learned quickly. Hunter planted its left foot and pulled its right arm back, delivering a devastating blow to the proprietor's face.

Frank's body slammed into the shelf, sending binoculars and a hidden bottle of Scotch crashing to the floor. The bottle shattered, spilling the whisky he had enjoyed after closing hours. Blood dripped from his nose onto his deer-print shirt as he watched helplessly. The shop bell jangled with unnatural cheer as the mannequin fled with the rifle.

Minutes later, two officers responded to Frank's frantic 911 call. They found the proprietor holding a bloodstained tissue to his nose.

"You've got to hurry! Don't let it get away!" His eyes were wild, as if his life had become a bizarre dreamscape.

Officer Morgan lowered the volume of his handheld radio. "Can you tell us what happened here?" he asked.

"I'm telling you. It's the most incredible thing I've ever seen," Frank said excitedly. "The thing grabbed the rifle right out of my hands and took off running!"

"Sir," the officer said firmly, "you need to slow down. You're not making any sense."

Frank rolled his eyes, biting back a retort. He paused to wipe his nose and grab another tissue, then said more calmly, "It all started when a laughing female mannequin ran into my shop—she wasn't really laughing, just had her mouth open like she was. She touched a mannequin that was kneeling on that display." He turned and pointed. "And when he came to life, he walked over to me, took my rifle, and ran out of the shop!"

Curiously, the second officer asked, "Did you say . . . a mannequin?"

"Yes!" Frank yelled, his voice strident. "A man-nequin. How much plainer can I be!"

"What is your name, sir?" the first officer asked.

"Frank Irving," he said matter-of-factly. "I'm the owner."

"Have you been drinking today?"

"No, I haven't been drinking! Do I sound like I've been drinking?"

The two officers gazed at each other, confirming identical thoughts.

"Why do I smell alcohol?"

"Because the thing struck me. It busted my lip and bloodied my nose!" Frank lowered the tissue from his face, revealing a swollen upper lip and a bloodied nose. "When I hit the shelf, several items fell, including a bottle of whisky," he shouted, waving at the mess.

The second officer scribbled notes, trying not to snicker at the implausible story. *Other officers have submitted strange reports*, he thought, *but this one takes the cake.* He looked up from his pad to ask, "How was the mannequin dressed?"

"He's wearing an expensive hunting outfit," Frank said, his expression begged: *Who will pay for that?*

Suppressing laughter, the officer asked, "Did he happen to say his name?"

Frank saw the officer smirking as he scribbled. His annoyance was palpable as the officer's flippant attitude pressed on. Frank's eyebrows shot up, his face contorting with a cascade of emotion. "As a matter of fact, he did! His name is Johnny Hunter!" he scoffed, his head jerking with each word.

Approaching Gables by the Sea.

The emergence of hundreds of mannequins unleashed a flood of terror across Miami, but none as horrific as the massive pileup on the southbound Palmetto Expressway, State Road 826, where thirty-four mannequins ran into traffic going the wrong way. They scattered into four lanes, their arms pumping as they ran, never tiring, never faltering. No heart to overwork. Their eerie eyes were fixed on the horizon, never blinking or shifting under the rush of the wind.

Horns blared and tires screeched as confused drivers swerved to avoid the pack of oncoming dummies, leading to twisted metal and shattered glass, audible from blocks away. The destruction worsened when a diesel truck plowed into the stalled cars, exploding in a huge fireball. Within minutes, the pileup left eighty-seven vehicles wrecked, fifty-seven injured, and nine dead before traffic came to a stop.

Southeasterly winds raced under a sweltering noon sun as seagulls hovered in a cloudless sky. They glided in looping circles, riding the wind. Drawn by curiosity, they lingered until thick black smoke twisted skyward and drove them off.

With the wild calls of seagulls fading, the mannequins navigated the chaos of mangled vehicles and injured passengers. The throng climbed over the twisted metal, deftly jumping from one crumpled car to another. After clearing the half-mile devastation, they ran between the lanes of motionless cars, white-lining with the precision of seasoned motorcycle riders. Their plastic faces and robotic movements stunned onlookers as they sprinted by. People scrambled out of their vehicles to watch as thirty-three mannequins sprinted north on the southbound highway.

"Hey, everyone," cried a woman at the forefront of the accident. Her hands flew to her cheeks in shock. "There's someone pinned underneath this car!"

Several men ran over and positioned themselves. On the count of three, they strained together to lift the front end as two others freed the injured man. Their faces buckled with disbelief as more people crowded around. The injured man lay crumpled beside his severed leg. His black leather shoes and suit were scuffed and torn after being dragged forty-five feet.

But the most gruesome detail wasn't the blood or bone. It was the headless image that lingered, as if time refused to move on.

The woman who had cried out for help fainted.

Unexpectedly, the body moved. Muttering ran through the crowd as everyone took an involuntary step back. The maimed figure felt the road with a white hand, scraping its fingertips against the rough asphalt. The tension thickened around them. Astonished, the crowd watched as the mannequin pushed up from the ground with both arms. After a moment's strain, it managed to stand on one leg, balanced like a pink flamingo in its natural habitat.

"What the heck?" someone said, backing away from the inexplicable specter.

Even though it had no head, just a stump of neck, the mangled figure recognized the presence of the people around it, clustering together to see the freak. It meant no harm. It merely wanted to seek out more of its kind and give life.

Attempting to run, the mannequin plunged forward onto its torso like a doomed science project, sparked into motion by crossed wires. With difficulty, it stood again, fearing nothing and aching to resume its mission, only to fall yet again. It failed to comprehend why it couldn't run with just one leg.

"Don't let him get away," someone yelled. "He's the cause of this accident!"

Two men lifted the mannequin to its feet and began pummeling it. With each blow, it jerked violently, but even on one leg, it learned to lash out. Mirroring its attackers' clenched fists, it swung forcefully, knocking one man into the others with an unexpected hook. Several other men jumped in to restrain its arms. Using their grips as anchors, the mannequin lifted its only leg and hurled a man with a swift kick to his chest, leaving him wheezing for breath.

"He's too strong!" someone shouted, his chest heaving. "Get fuel, now!"

Within seconds, the mannequin was engulfed, spasming in fire until nothing moved but smoke.

Miami International Airport.

A solitary dummy bolted down the curbside pickup area, startling a cluster of jet-lagged passengers still dazed from recent landings.

One woman inhaled sharply, clutching her purse. "What is that thing?!"

Their astonishment rippled through the crowd as the mannequin whizzed by in stonewashed jeans and a sports shirt. Many watched in wonder, as if seeing an extraterrestrial. Little did they know how right they were.

Caught off guard by the commotion, a taxi driver craned over his shoulder and rear-ended the car ahead. Oblivious to the fender bender, the second driver stumbled out, his bulging eyes tracking the disturbing figure.

"The white zone is for immediate loading and unloading of passengers only," the overhead speaker droned. Automated doors slid shut behind the mannequin as it disappeared into the terminal. Drawn by the spectacle, a large crowd trailed the unholy one at a safe distance. People jostled and shoved like paparazzi in pursuit of an international superstar. Women and children shrieked, and men stepped back with bewildered expressions as the tardy dummy sprinted past like a late traveler chasing a gate.

Retrieving their luggage from the conveyor belt, a couple peered toward the rising chaos. Like everyone else, they were astonished to see a mannequin flash past them.

"You see," the husband grumbled, hiking up his pants. "I told you vacationing in Miami was a bad idea. This kind of thing only happens in Florida."

"Shut up, Howard."

Hundreds of mannequins surged through the city streets, flexing synthetic limbs like marathon sprinters, driven to multiply. Their heads bobbed with each step, eyes locked in narrow tunnel vision, never flinching or blinking. Except for a few dummies sporting forged smiles, their expressions were stone-hard, giving no hint of what bizarre thoughts might be going through their minds.

Then, like spores caught in a seismic wind, they multiplied. What began in the downtown veins spilled into highways and suburbs, with thousands streaming faster and farther, emitting a low hum that tunneled into civilians' minds. The farther they spread, the quicker they bred, spreading like the perennial wildfires of Southern California.

Shopping centers and malls across Miami succumbed to a paralyzing outbreak of living mannequins. They emerged in grotesque variety: some clothed, some bare; some with heads, others topped with smooth neck stumps; some ambled on full-length limbs, while others staggered on truncated arms. A spectrum of synthetic hair: painted, curled, braided, and bearded, adorned their molded scalps. Dummies in business suits mingled with models in sleek evening gowns and teenagers in tight blouses and designer jeans. From the lingerie departments emerged the most provocative figures: mannequins clad in sheer teddies, chemises, bridal sets, and bustiers. Rather than triggering terror, they stirred catcalls and whistles from gawking onlookers.

A brave man had the temerity to accost a lingerie mannequin from the South Nautical Mall. It stood before him in a black see-through teddy, shameless and bold, as licentious thoughts ran through his head. For a moment, he swore its sapphire eyes stared back, unblinking. His eyes gorged on its long, feathered blonde hair and succulent, rosy lips, but it gave no response to his leers. His fingers trailed down its face and lingered on the smooth breasts, enjoying the silken texture. Though the flesh wasn't soft like a living woman's, it was still luscious. His eyes traced the sensuous curve of its inviting thighs before focusing on its virgin nipples.

Practically drooling, he fondled the lacy fabric and asked, "What are you doing tonight?"

✶ ✶ ✶

Doral, Miami-Dade County.

A mannequin with large, sad eyes under a brown bob that played in the wind exited the Palmetto Expressway at NW 36th Street and turned left on NW 72nd Avenue, causing a stir as it ran through the intersection. Dressed in black yoga pants and a sleeveless striped top, Cute Cindy headed east on NW 51st Street into an industrial district. Curious pedestrians followed at a safe distance until it stopped in front of a mannequin manufacturing plant.

A pedestrian door stood ajar beside a closed dock door. Cindy jogged up the ramp and stepped confidently inside, unfazed by the turmoil unfolding in the parking lot. Standing still by the metal door, it observed hundreds of skin-toned dummies, naked and aligned in rows of ten, stretching as far as its olive-green eyes could see. Each row held five expressionless females and five equally impassive males, all devoid of facial features.

Ashanti wore her glasses low on the bridge of her nose, pushing them up only to read. She stepped through the office door into the warehouse. "What the?" she mumbled, noticing the solitary dummy standing by the dock door. Her eyes scanned the area. "Okay, who's the practical joker?" she shouted, her brown eyes narrowing. No one answered. No one ever did. Ashanti exhaled sharply, shaking her head. *What a bunch of witless wonders!* Clipboard tucked under her arm, she stalked toward the meticulously dressed mannequin, wig and all. She scrutinized its facial features, scrunching her nose at the shoddy craftsmanship. "This isn't one of ours."

The mysterious figure flexed its fingers surreptitiously.

Sweeping her gaze over the crowd in the parking lot, Ashanti wondered whether it was safe to leave the door open. She could see the crowd gesturing and shouting, but couldn't make out their cries over the clanking and pounding on the production floor. She slammed the door shut and locked it, missing the subtle tilt of the dummy's head.

Balancing the figure under her left arm, Ashanti strode across the floor until Cute Cindy wriggled against her grip, its plastic body writhing like an Alaskan salmon swimming upstream.

She froze, her grip slackening as the mannequin twitched again.

Cute Cindy turned to face Ashanti with a cold, lifeless stare that sent shivers down her spine. Her breath caught. "Aaagh!" she screamed, instinctively releasing her hold. The large doll clunked on the floor.

Several workers in navy jumpsuits ran over.

Tall Jackson was the first to reach her. "Are you okay, Ashanti? What happened?"

"The mannequin . . . It came to life in my hands!" she cried, the hairs on her arms standing on end. Her hands shook as she backed away, unable to tear her eyes from the lifeless figure on the floor.

They looked at one another, baffled, and then their gaze fell upon the mannequin. The doll lay on its side, its head turned toward Ashanti as if listening. There was nothing unusual about it except that it wore the latest fashion and a short brown wig.

Then the creature jerked.

Its legs pumped in place, running but getting nowhere. The three warehousemen jumped back in surprise while others kept their distance. Ashanti's breath caught in her throat before she screamed again.

Tall Jackson said through hysterical peals of laughter, "That's a mechanical mannequin!" He patted her shoulder, comforting his trembling supervisor. "I've heard about these battery-operated dummies." His eyes watered as his tall frame shook with mirth. The other two workers joined in, laughing at Ashanti's expense as she began to feel small and insignificant. She smiled meekly, avoiding her coworkers' mocking eyes.

Before anyone could speak again, the mannequin twisted. Setting both hands against the cement floor, it pulled its legs in and stood flawlessly.

There's nothing mechanical about that! T.J. thought.

They held their breath, seeing but not believing, until Ashanti couldn't take the strain any longer. She shrieked and bolted for the exit door, clipboard tumbling away, arms flailing like an inflatable tube man. Her hands shook as she fumbled with the rusty handle—a long overdue OSHA violation. After ramming it repeatedly, she gave up and struck the large red button, causing the dock door to roll up. Drenched in sweat, Ashanti burst through the opening, barreling down the ramp toward the crowd in the parking lot.

T.J. gaped. The doll he had called mechanical crept forward, its arms reaching out as if to carry him across the floor like the supervisor had.

"Get your hands off me!" he screamed. Jackson bashed the female mannequin in the face several times. Learning from this predicament, Cute Cindy struck back with equal precision, pounding his face and driving him back with explosive blows.

"¡Apártate!" A short, stocky man with a thick mustache sprang into action. *¡Ninguna máquina podría realizar tal maniobra!* He swung at the dummy with a 2x4, clobbering it across the face several times and knocking it to the floor. The mannequin lay on its left side with its right leg scissored forward, fists still clenched. Benjamin gasped, his lips quivering as his wild eyes landed on the torn jaw. The mere sight of the maimed doll gave him goosebumps. Thinking the worst was over, he dropped the 2x4.

The day crew clapped and cheered at the outcome, relieved that he had killed whatever it was. Jackson pounded Benjamin's back and shouted, "You did it, mi amigo! You killed the devil!"

Whack!

A blow to the head sent Benjamin to the floor. His jaundiced eyes focused on the perfectly aligned warehouse lights and galvanized ducts. Cindy stood over him, holding the 2x4 like a batter on deck. Its lower jaw dangled like a broken drawer, but it displayed no pain. No longer cute, Cindy did what it had been taught. It raised the 2x4 over its head and bludgeoned the convulsing man, splitting his skull until he breathed no more. Every worker stormed out the dock door and down the ramp, never looking back.

Amid the chaos, the machines roared on, hissing, cutting, stamping in relentless cadence. Conveyor belts groaned and clacked, their industrial chorus echoing the frenetic pulse of Grand Central Station at rush hour.

Still holding the bloodied 2x4 like a new appendage, Cindy turned rigidly and walked toward the first row of newly manufactured dummies, its narrow nose jutting past a dangling jaw. Five hundred mannequins stood before it. The moment Cindy touched the first one, an electric spark leapt between them, igniting a chain reaction. Daughter cells multiplied, transferring their

DNA to trillions of cells, giving life to the artificial being. The naked mannequin tilted its head, taking in its surroundings. Sensing the presence of another mannequin, it grasped the other's arm. Gradually, each dummy reached for the next, until every figure had gained life.

In eerie unison, they held each other's hands for balance and placed one foot in front of the other. Tentative movements lengthened into confident strides, accelerating like a locomotive. The echo of five hundred synchronized feet reverberated through the warehouse. Within seconds, the horde of neonate mannequins surged toward the dock door where Cindy had vanished.

Neither proud nor pleased about bearing so many children, Cindy jogged down the ramp into the unruly crowd, its impassive eyes staring straight ahead.

Huddled with the rest of the crew, Jackson suddenly pointed. "There she is! The murderer is getting away!"

A mob closed in on Cindy, unleashing a flurry of blows and kicks, but nothing seemed to affect the creature. It didn't cry out or recoil from the brutality. Jackson glared at the mannequin before driving his fist into its face. With a fury, he hurled it into the chain-link fence. The 2x4 clattered to the pavement as Cindy lost her grip, rebounding into his waiting arms.

Someone from the crowd shouted, "Gawd, would ya look at that!"

With their backs to the warehouse, everyone turned to look. Their jaws dropped, disbelief shimmering in their eyes.

Unashamed in their nakedness, a host of mannequins were mid-way down the ramp in flawless formation, their plastic feet in perfect step like a well-trained brigade.

One, two, three, four.

One, two, three, four.

They watched Cindy's mistreatment unfold—each blow, each insult absorbed in silence. Under the beating sun, they studied technique: stance, pivot, follow-through. What had once been passive observation became preparation. Arms once molded for display curled into fists. Legs bent, ready for impact.

Then came the loud lunch whistle, slicing through the air like the bell that starts a bout. It wasn't meant for them, but they took it as a signal. A cue. A call to arms.

No longer props, but contenders entering the ring, the mannequins bolted in unison. Their movements were stiff yet purposeful, driven not by instinct but by imitation. They had learned enough.

Panic rippled through the crowd. People scattered, heedless of one another, desperate to escape the throng of living dummies. For many, it became a lesson not soon forgotten. Kicks and blows landed with mechanical precision. Several men were hurled into the chain-link fence, rebounding into fresh punishment.

Though he'd endured the sting of a naked angel tattoo on his left calf, Alden was about to discover real pain. Faced with the advancing army, he danced and dodged, showing off the fancy footwork he had learned as an amateur boxer and lashed out at the closest mannequin with a double jab, right cross, left hook, and another right cross. The figure recoiled as each strike hit home, but quickly assimilated the boxer's techniques. Then it executed its fancy footwork. Not as agile as Alden, its attempt was mediocre.

The boxer laughed. "You've got to be fuckin' kidding me," he said, lowering his guard. Without warning, the mannequin lashed out with a double jab, right cross, left hook, and another right cross to his face. It kicked Alden in the groin, doubling him over in agony. His face turned purple, eyes glazed as he gasped for air. Only a dry wheeze escaped his throat before he toppled over, unconscious.

Ignorant of their victory, the mannequins darted in different directions, searching for more of their kind. Cindy headed southeast, clutching the 2x4 it had come to rely on.

Unaware of the danger lurking outside the hotel room, Nolan sat quietly in bed wearing only a tank top, his skinny hairy legs tucked under the sheets. He stared at the cheap oil painting of the Grand Canal in Venice. As the brushstrokes blurred, his mind drifted back to the hotel lobby earlier that day, to where he stood at the front desk, Dolores eyeing the candy rack. Nolan had met her at a grocery store nearly four months ago, and he had begun to wonder how much longer he could afford their weekly rendezvous. The room on the ground floor had cost him $69.95, plus tax. "I only have forty-five dollars on me. Do you have any money?" he had asked, his voice barely above a whisper, eyes avoiding hers.

Dolores's belittling gaze cut through him as she chewed on a stick of gum like a contented cow chewing cud. "Why can't you just use your credit card?" she had said in a nasal tone.

Nolan had given her a miserly smile and paid with a card, leaving further evidence for his suspicious wife, who would eventually use the receipt in a divorce case.

"After this, I want you to take me to the supermarket to get some groceries," she had said, sliding into bed naked. She gave him an insincere peck on the cheek to soften the financial blow and reached for the remote control.

Now, with Dolores flipping through the channels beside him and laughing at smidgens of *I Love* Lucy reruns, Nolan caught sight of her 15-millimeter mole on her thigh that he found repulsive. It was dark and lumpy, with a single hair sprouting from its center.

A scuffle outside the hotel room caught his attention. It was nothing new in this part of town, mainly since the hotel was next to a bar. He sat up in bed, turning his left ear toward the window and furrowing his brows in concentration. As the scuffle grew louder, the thin canvas shook after someone or something slammed into the wall, and based on the commotion, Nolan guessed three or four people were struggling outside their window.

Dolores lowered the television volume.

A crash shattered the calm, scattering shards like glittering, deadly confetti. Someone landed with a thud at the foot of the bed. Dolores screamed, shielding herself with the sheets as Nolan yanked the covers over his head like a frightened child. Outside, retreating footsteps echoed as the perpetrators fled after flinging some poor soul in their room.

Flapping wildly like an angry goose, the vertical blinds settled into eerie silence. Nolan peered out from the bed sheet with Dolores painfully still next to him, her knuckles pale and rigid, pleating the sheet with silent panic.

A hand appeared at the foot of the bed, groping for a hold like a ghoul clawing its way out of a grave. Using the mattress for leverage, a male figure rose, the broad brim of a ten-gallon hat shading a pale, unreadable face. He wore an embroidered shirt, jeans, and a black leather belt with "America" engraved on the gaudy bronze buckle. The man lifted his dimpled chin, revealing plastic-coated features, and moved its head mechanically like an industrial robot. Through fiberglass eyes, it saw the lovers bathed in an orange tint, its stare cold and indifferent.

When Dolores lifted her gaze, her pupils dilated, and her hands began to tremble. At first, she remained silent. But when she realized the man was a walking mannequin, she screamed in terror. She yanked the sheets off and dashed out of the room, wearing nothing but a terrified look.

Nolan hunched on the bed, languishing in a pool of hot urine. Blood dripped from the knuckles of his right hand, where his teeth had gouged the skin.

After watching Dolores bolt for the door, the cowboy turned and jumped out the window in search of more mannequins, sending the blinds flapping wildly again.

* * *

Evelyn dragged her son out of the car, her grip firm with urgency. The keys jingled in her trembling hand as she unlocked the apartment door. Herman shouted in protest when she yanked him inside—an uncharacteristic burst of desperation she didn't have time to explain. It was only a matter of time before the plastic plague consumed Miami, its chaos spilling outward, infecting neighborhoods, igniting panic, poised to engulf every state and, in time, the globe.

After ensuring she hadn't been followed, Evelyn slammed the door shut, letting out a sigh of relief. It was the first time she could catch her breath, but her heart still burned.

Herman gave her a puzzled look. His innocent mind had seen no trouble. It was all fun and games to him. He had no clue what he'd set in motion, and there was no way to scold him or make him understand he'd just changed the world forever.

Before he could say a word, Evelyn was off and running again. She scrambled between their bedrooms, flinging clothes and toiletries into a large suitcase. The Mr. Cow photo and letter he'd written last Christmas, still tucked in the drawer, stayed behind. After thirty minutes, she hauled the bag out into the living room, where Herman stood with a blank expression. Not letting up, she opened the closet door and tugged the string. Light spilled into the room, catching the twin dolls as they strolled out of the shadows. They looked up at her, their arms reaching for affection. "I'm afraid there's no time for that now," she said, grabbing the dolls and making the voice mechanism squeak. She stuffed them between two pairs of jeans and zipped up the suitcase.

Evelyn glanced at her watch, the ticking second hand sharpening her urgency. "Did you use the bathroom?"

Herman nodded, but anchored himself to the spot, pulling back against her grip on his arm. With her free hand, she dragged the suitcase to the door.

"Hat." He pointed at his toy chest.

"Not now, Herman," she said impatiently. "We have to go!"

"Want hat."

"But you already have a jester hat!" she raised her voice.

Herman's eyes were glassy and his lower lip quivered. "Want other one," he sniveled.

Evelyn breathed in slowly, aware now of her harshness. "All right then. Go get one." Her voice softened, and she smiled. It was something she hadn't done since the incident at the department store. *It wasn't his fault. None of this would have happened if I had kept a closer eye on him.*

Herman ran to the toy chest and rooted through its contents. Action figures and board games tumbled out, creating a cheerful mess. The squeak of a rubber ducky echoed playfully against the tinkling notes of the jack-in-the-box. A grin spread across his face when he found the hat he wanted.

In a fresh panic, Evelyn seized his wrist and stormed out, locking the door behind her. The suitcase rattled down the stairs, its uneven cadence merging with the sounds of the bustling street.

She reached the car and threw the suitcase into the trunk. Moments later, Evelyn sped out of the driveway, sweat beading on her brow as she cut off a red sedan. The driver slammed the brakes, and though she couldn't hear his words, his obscene gestures made his frustration clear. Determined to fly out of Fort Lauderdale, she tightened her grip and pressed harder on the gas.

Driving north, she saw signs of chaos: shattered storefronts, upturned mannequins tangled in seaweed, the distant wail of sirens echoing through salt-thick air. Sadly, street gangs also took this opportunity to loot and vandalize establishments. The glare of brake lights snapped her attention back to the road.

"Great," she said, jamming her foot on the brake pedal. "Now what?" Her car stopped behind other vehicles.

Excited, Herman leaned forward in his seat. "Crash!"

Two cars had collided at the intersection ahead. *Probably caused by a mannequin,* she thought. Evelyn exhaled hard, realizing she might be stuck for a while. She hit the horn. "Come on! Move it!"

A group gathered on the sidewalk, gesturing wildly, their voices sharp with alarm. They were pointing at something down the street, where sirens had begun wailing. One by one, they crouched. Hands scraped the pavement, snatching up rocks, bottles, chunks of crumbled asphalt. Debris arced through the air, whipping past Evelyn's car.

Herman's head tilted back, following the rocks' trajectory. "Beautiful people," he said softly.

Evelyn's heart skipped a beat. Her frightened eyes stared into the rearview mirror and saw three mannequins sprinting up the street.

A rock hurtled through the air and struck one on the head. The impact left a small dent, but the dummy didn't flinch. Dressed in khaki and a red shirt, it bent down, grabbed the offending stone with its smooth, flesh-colored hand, and hurled it back.

Evelyn screamed as the rock shattered her rear windshield. She threw the gear into reverse and glanced over her shoulder just as her son's fingers knotted in her hair.

"Herman, no!" she yelled in pain.

"Beautiful people!" he yelled, afraid she wouldn't let him play with his friends.

Evelyn pried at his fingers, the car jerking as her foot wavered between the accelerator and brake pedals. Herman clawed at her face with one hand.

"Stop it, Herman!" she begged, her voice cracking. "We need to get out of here!" She slapped his hands away and pushed him aside, guilt clawing at her.

The tires squealed as Evelyn slammed it into drive and punched the accelerator. Fueled by raw determination, she cut into a driveway and barreled down the sidewalk, horn blaring. Pedestrians scattered, diving into bushes as she tore past.

"Play with beautiful people!" Herman's tantrum escalated, his fists pounding on the door panel as he kicked the dashboard.

When Evelyn careened back onto the street, the bumper scraped the asphalt with a grating noise and a shower of sparks. Air whipped through the window, tousling Herman's hair as his fury faltered—blown thin like smoke. Her grip tightened as she spotted a crowd beating a lone mannequin. The crack of plastic limbs hitting concrete triggered a queasy twist in her gut.

"Herman, close your window," she said firmly.

Pressing the button, Herman watched the window ascend, his gaze climbing with it.

As Evelyn turned left onto Flagler Street, a surge of people spilled into her path. Heart racing, she slammed the brakes. The tires screeched just inches from the mob. She exhaled slowly, thankful no one had been hurt.

"That's odd," she murmured, scanning the sea of faces. Evelyn leaned forward, locking eyes with her suspicious neighbor, Olivia Sanders. She offered a polite smile, but something in Olivia's demeanor made Evelyn's skin crawl.

"That's him! He's the one!" Olivia shouted, pointing at Herman, who sat clueless in the passenger seat. She grabbed the man next to her and pushed him forward. "Do something! He's the one who gave life to the mannequins!" Olivia exclaimed, thinking back to when her son had told her about the two walking dolls.

Evelyn couldn't believe what she'd heard. Her

neighbor betrayed her, barely blinking. *How could she have known?*

Already in a murderous frenzy, the man marched toward the car's passenger side, the threads of his torn-off denim sleeves brushing against the wind. He slammed his face against the window, shouting profanities and pounding his fist into a cupped palm.

Facing a new threat, Evelyn locked the doors and shifted the car in reverse, but the crowd had already swarmed around them. She gasped as the man yanked on the door handle, his fury mounting with each failed attempt.

After he kicked the window to no avail, another man put a restraining hand on his arm. "Taylor, you're taking this too far! Just let them be, for goodness' sake!"

An unexpected shove sent his friend hurtling to the ground. "I'm not going to sit around and let this happen to my town!" Taylor shouted. He whirled around and kicked the window with brute force. Glass burst into glittering shards, spraying the seat and slicing Herman's cheek. His violent display incited others to join the mayhem.

Several people began rocking the car, their hands gripping the frame as they tried to flip it over. The vehicle groaned under the strain. Evelyn's head knocked against the window. She winced, searching the crowd for a sympathetic face.

"Help us," she called out, voice cracking as she clung to the steering wheel. "Someone, please help!"

Herman whimpered beside her, pawing at the cuts on his face. A man leaped onto the hood, denting the metal with each step. Then, out of the corner of her eye, she saw Taylor reach through the shattered window and unfasten Herman's seatbelt. Her breath caught. She lunged forward, arms outstretched, trying to pull her son back.

"Stop!" she cried, voice raw.

Herman's legs slid through the window as her fingers grazed his ankle, then nothing. Just the blur of movement and the sting of tears clouding her vision.

Olivia continued to incite the crowd, her face flushed with rage. "Don't let them get away!" Her voice boomed through the melee as she steered them toward the blocked car.

Evelyn jumped out to retrieve her son, ignoring Olivia's cries for justice. She chased Herman's cries, yelling, "Leave my son alone!" No one listened.

Herman cried out, fists pummeling Taylor's grip as he was dragged up the courthouse steps.

"So, you're the one who brought the mannequins to life!" Taylor shouted, his gaze sharp and unflinching.

Herman tried to explain. "Beautiful people," he moaned through his tears.

To the crowd, Herman's tears were just anguish— but they were a beacon for help. Some mannequins were hours away, others mere minutes, but they all felt the immediate pull. From Leisure City to Cooper City, every mannequin paused in its mission and responded to the lifegiver's distress.

The crowd, growing louder and rowdier, chanted, "Burn the freak! Burn the freak!"

Her hair in shambles, Evelyn ran up the steps and stood on the landing, overlooking the frantic crowd. She held her arms out, beseeching the mob to see reason. "My son is not a troublemaker! He's simply curious!" Her voice, ragged and thunderous, crashed against deaf ears as the crowd surrounded Taylor and her son, vitriol spitting from their angry faces.

As Taylor raised his fist to strike, a sharp wooden thud cracked against the back of his head. The world spun as he stumbled backward, collapsing onto the stairs, eyes fixed and face twisted in a grimace of pain.

Disfigured Cindy stood over him with the same bloodstained 2x4 that Benjamin had used. Its face was blank, showing no emotion for having saved its lifegiver. The tear in its jaw had widened from the crowd's clawing fingers, and the protrusion jiggled like a loose bicycle fender with each step.

For one suspended beat, silence reigned. Then a young man with a bucket hat tackled Cindy, and a surge of bodies followed, fists and boots raining down. The hat flew off as he seized Cindy by the torn jaw and forced it to stand.

"Stand back, everyone!" someone shouted. The 2x4 sliced through the air and struck the pummeled dummy in the head, ripping it off and sending it tumbling down the steps like a rogue bowling ball veering across multiple lanes.

Fifteen or twenty mannequins lay motionless, already fallen in their attempt to rescue the boy who gave them life. Seeing the defenders unresponsive, the crowd turned their attention back to the helpless boy. Evelyn, clutching her frightened child, fell to her knees.

"Please don't hurt my son!" she cried, shielding him with her arm. "He meant no harm!"

The crowd refused to listen. They converged again, intent on retribution. A man pointed at Herman. "We need to end this right now!"

But before the crowd could act, a ripple of unease ran through them. Their voices faded, one by one, until no more cries of hatred lingered in their lungs. A blanket of confusion settled over them as they stood alert, ears perked like meerkats in the grasslands of southern Africa.

They heard it . . . and so did Evelyn.

It sounded like an approaching locomotive or the feet of ten thousand marathon runners coming from every direction. Fear washed over the crowd as they twisted and turned, scanning the streets for the source of the noise—until it was too late.

They appeared everywhere, bursting at the seams in the fabric of life. Showing no fatigue, thousands of mannequins stampeded through the streets toward the courthouse steps. Many were dressed in the latest fashion, while others were stark naked, attracting stupefied expressions from civilians. Within seconds, the crowd found itself encircled. No exits, no mercy.

On Flagler Street, mayhem erupted under a clear sky.

Maybe the raging bull on Ethan's T-shirt drove him to charge in without thinking. It cost him his life. Grabbing the 2x4, he battered a few mannequins. With every swing, the board sliced through the air. He ducked to avoid a punch, letting the 2x4's momentum guide his next move. The board arced upward, smashing a mannequin's face and dropping it cold. Ethan had the upper hand, but his mouth dropped open in disbelief when he turned to face his next assailant.

Before him stood the mannequin from the Japanese store. It wore Japanese armor from the Oda Nobunaga era, with vertical plates across the torso and a crest on its helmet. Ethan flinched as the samurai showed off its footwork and newly acquired one-handed techniques. How it had learned kenjutsu remained a mystery, but the blood on its blade spoke of violence in a martial arts school. Emulating the moves of a legendary samurai master, the mannequin swiftly drew a sword and aligned its wrist behind the blade handle. At the last instant, its elbow joint snapped forward, the blade dragging in a brutal arc designed for maximum damage . . .

The automated Metromover 15 had just pulled away from Government Center Station, where a large crowd stood quietly. Nearby, the escalator hummed as Johnny Hunter emerged from its depths. First came the gleaming tip of its rifle, piercing the earth's surface. Then, slowly, the mannequin's hooded head rose into view. As Johnny fully appeared, it deftly stepped off the moving staircase, its boots gripping the comb plate. Several people recoiled at the sight of a rifle. But when they realized it was a walking mannequin, panic erupted. They screamed and rushed into the station, pressing behind the glass doors, huddling for safety as a crowd of stunned onlookers gathered.

Johnny Hunter stood at the edge of the landing beneath a waffle-iron ceiling. With nowhere else to go but down, it scanned both directions before leaping off the 3-foot ledge, its camouflaged boots gripping the Brickell Loop tracks. It stepped over the guide rail and ran south on the Downtown Loop tracks without wasting time. Passing several Metrorail support pillars, it felt the rumblings of the northbound train braking to a stop above it. Johnny could see the skyline ahead, but it meant nothing. The sun's warmth—a distant cousin—was more appealing than anything this world offered . . .

For the first time in Miami's history, mayhem flooded Flagler Street and spilled into surrounding neighborhoods with a vengeance. People and mannequins clashed in a frenzy, fists flying without pause.

In frustration, a man wearing a guayabera grabbed his short, curly hair and tried to calm the mob, "¡Señoras y señores, no se asusten! ¡Mantengan la calma!"

"¿Qué demonios es esto?" someone else cried before fleeing.

A swarm of forty mannequins quickly surrounded the lifegiver, shielding him from the mob, their blows landing with eerie precision. Herman danced in the center of his safe zone, elated to be among friends instead of being dragged around by that nasty man who wanted to hurt him. He writhed and jerked to imagined music. Each time he jumped, he snorted like a wild beast. The antlers on his moose hat bobbled with each ecstatic leap, mimicking a sparring buck in rut.

Johnny Hunter stopped running. Remembering the massive hunting mural, the mannequin thought it saw the greatest prize of all. And sure enough, there it stood, about three hundred feet away. A bona fide, gorgeous moose bucking ecstatically and making beautiful grunting sounds! It was just like the mural. The pose. The distance. The thrill. The hunter aimed, peered into the riflescope . . . and fired.

It was the shot heard across Miami. When the lifegiver hit the ground, the mannequins dropped with him, from the outer reaches of the city to the concentrated center where Herman's body lay. The streets fell silent, as if the city itself had gone dark.

Then came the high-frequency yawp, undetectable to the human ear. Each mannequin released a final shriek that echoed through empty alleys and high-rise towers. The sound threaded through every mind, bursting the protective bubbles with mannequin-related memories. Every trace of this historic day dissolved, leaving a void of confusion.

Evelyn had built her life around contingencies, but losing her son had never been part of her plan. "No!" she wailed. Her son lay lifeless, his legs bent out of shape and his eyes appallingly still. Huddled on the rough concrete steps, she gathered his limp body, rocking him as her voice trembled with endearments and grief.

One could bend pain, twist it out of shape, and alter its perception, and it would still register as agony. Add deep colors, dark red and raven black, and it becomes torment. Evelyn's torment was captured on canvas with splashes of grief. In that haunting spectrum, the universe lost a son.

The last mannequin toppled over, landing on an endless sea of fiberglass bodies. Flagler Street had become a cemetery of lifeless forms stretching into the distance. The bond between Herman and the mannequins had vanished. No yearning remained. No urge to flourish or seek others of their kind. The passion had extinguished.

As the confused crowd stood on the courthouse steps, scratching their heads and scanning the chaos, a grim realization began to settle: civilians had been injured, some brutally murdered. They looked to one another for answers, wondering how they'd ended up here, in the heart of downtown Miami. No one could remember a thing. Where had the mannequins come from? Why were they scattered across the streets, so many of them battered and broken? These and other unspoken questions churned through their minds.

One perk Governor Arthur J. Townsend enjoyed was reading the next day's headlines before they reached the public, streamed in real time through the steady clatter of his office teletype. But at 5:30 that afternoon, he sighed heavily as a frown formed. Now in his second term, Arthur sat back in his swivel chair, tapping his upper lip as he savored a Dominican cigar. Through his half-rim glasses, he peered at the thin paper curling out of the machine beside him, each line stamped with outlandish headlines: "City of the Dead," "Invasion of the Mannequins," "The Dead Walk Among Us," and "Are Friends Fiberglass?" Every outlet had picked up the story, clueless about what had happened.

Sure, Florida was known for weird and unusual stories, but Arthur never remembered seeing anything like this. Editorial pages brimmed with requests for the public's help to explain the phenomenon. Despite dozens of interviews and countless reporters out on the beat, no one could unravel the mystery. Even with the promise of being named a state hero and given the keys to the city. One person did know the answer to all the questions. Evelyn Sinclair. And she wasn't talking. Not for fame, not for safety, not for anyone.

Arthur had called an emergency meeting in his Tallahassee office. Puffing furiously on his cigar, he turned his irate gaze on each staff member in turn. He waved a stack of teletype headlines. "Are you telling me not one fuckin' idiot can remember what happened in four hours?" he barked, as if they'd personally penned the cringeworthy columns. He was starving for answers, and every time he puffed on his cigar, not one cloud of smoke satisfied his appetite. "Even I remember stubbing my toe at two o'clock in the morning! Give me a break!"

Within an hour, the governor made his position unmistakably clear: every newspaper in Miami was to scrap the mannequin story. He couldn't stomach the idea of the nation thinking Florida was full of inept fools. Better to sweep the whole episode under the rug than invite national ridicule. Under pressure from the governor's office, Miami's editors folded. The mannequin story was buried. In its place, headlines spoke of a citywide festival gone awry and the massive cleanup that followed. People could dig through the archives all they wanted. They'd find no trace of the day the mannequins came to life.

After the final call, and once the staff had gone home, Arthur stood at the window, admiring the trees outside his Capitol office. As usual during crises, Lieutenant Governor Nate McFadden stood quietly behind him. His pleather shoes squeaked with each shift of weight.

Arthur couldn't stop thinking about the mannequins and the deaths that defied explanation. The questions haunted him.

Could the mannequins have come to life to cause chaos and destruction? Were they figments of imagination, triggered by a gas leak or fumes from the sewage system? Perhaps they were never alive to begin with. Only God knows how many secrets the mind holds.

The governor puffed on his cigar, exhaling from his sour mouth. "A wise man once said," he remarked, his eyes fixed on the red sunset.

"What's that?" Nate replied.

"Imagination is the secret."

✳ ✳ ✳

Tuesday, September 30, 1980.

Knowing she and Herman had lived too little intensified Evelyn's sense of loss. Feeling the weight of a cruel and unforgiving world, she walked to her apartment, oversized sunglasses hiding her red, puffy eyes. Her cherished off-white cardigan offered fragile comfort, softening the anguish radiating from her funeral dress.

As she stepped into her apartment, a wave of relief washed over her. The door clicked shut, followed by the heavy thud of the deadbolt. In the quiet sanctuary of her home, her son's presence embraced her. From the bronze baby shoes atop the television to the photographs cluttering every surface, his spirit lingered.

Tossing her keys onto the kitchen counter, she picked up one of her most treasured pictures. It was a snapshot of Herman dancing in his whimsical cow hat, twirling blissfully to the beat of his favorite new-wave song. His laughter rang in her mind as she relived the joy of jumping and dancing beside him. His memories were like a flickering flame—offering warmth even in her darkest hours. *I would do it all over again, just for the chance to hold his hands and hear his infectious laughter.*

She smiled.

And now he was gone.

The aroma of stale coffee lingered, mingling with the quiet ache that filled the room. As she bowed her head and closed her eyes, a single tear slipped down her cheek. *If given the chance*, she sighed as she wiped away the tear, *I would fill his life with more laughter. And with greater vigilance, let him explore the world he so seldom saw.*

In the days leading up to the funeral, Evelyn had been thinking about leaving Miami, going somewhere far from Flagler Street and those dreadful, coldhearted steps of the courthouse. She longed to vanish, to escape to a new community where nothing strange ever happened. *Someplace,* she mused, *like Koreatown, Los Angeles.*

After slipping into her nightgown, Evelyn moved her rocking chair beside the lamp, where the dim light illuminated the sparsely furnished room. Her slippers flapped against the floor as she moved. Then she opened the closet door and beckoned. "Come here, my little ones."

The two dolls wobbled into the light. They reached their arms up, pleading to be carried. Evelyn bent down, lifted both dolls, and cradled them tenderly in her arms.

"Don't worry, my darlings," she said, docking into the rocking chair. "No one will ever hurt you." Her feet pushed against the floor, rocking the old wooden chair. The gentle creak of the old wood soothed her grief.

The dolls stared impassively at Evelyn, their round blue eyes blinking mechanically, their faces devoid of a smile. They ran their tiny hands through her hair. Evelyn felt a flicker of gratitude that the dolls had not met the same fate as the mannequins. *Is it because they're made of rubber instead of polyethylene?* she wondered. They patted her tear-ridden cheeks lovingly, then paused. Their touch grew deliberate, as though grief had taught them tenderness. With the help of the weighted mechanism crier, they whispered, "Mama."

Thursday, October 2, 1980.

In the days following the melee, garbage trucks rumbled through Miami's streets, scooping up the mannequins like battlefield casualties. Governor Townsend had ordered their immediate removal, hoping to erase the spectacle from public memory. For weeks, the dummies sat in a cavernous recycling facility, surrounded by the groan of conveyor belts and the hiss of pneumatic arms. Fluorescent lights buzzed overhead, casting a sterile glow over the two mounds of mannequins. The first mound held mutilated dummies with torn limbs and ripped garments; the other, perfectly intact mannequins that had perished en route to the courthouse steps.

Department store adjusters and hired workers sifted through the mounds, tossing salvageable mannequins into the backs of pickup trucks. The scene was too bizarre to ignore. Workers couldn't resist snapping pictures with the dummies, grinning beside their frozen companions like tourists in a wax museum.

"Look, everyone!" shouted a man in work gloves, stumbling backward. His voice cracked as he pointed at a figure near the edge of the mound. "This mannequin is pregnant!"

The crowd converged, boots crunching over broken plastic. As their eyes fell upon the figure, chatter turned to whispers. A female mannequin lay flat on its back, its see-through teddy splayed open over its protruding belly. Its sales tag traced back to the lingerie department at Nautical South Mall. The same place where a man of flesh and blood had once interrupted its eerie stride down a corridor. Its synthetic blonde hair was swept to the side, held by an elastic headband. Pink lips and glassy sapphire eyes gave it a disturbingly lifelike expression.

The belly twitched.

In unison, they gasped. Someone fainted. Then the mannequin's belly convulsed. A kick. A thrash. A sudden rupture. A gush of amniotic fluid splashed across someone's boots.

ACKNOWLEDGMENTS

Lifegiver was written between 2006 and 2008, long before the emergence of AI-assisted writing tools. In 2024, the author embraced these innovations to enhance the manuscript through selective drafting and editorial refinement. This manuscript reflects a collaborative process between the author and AI-assisted, with all final decisions and narrative direction remaining solely the author's.

I want to thank my beta reader and copy editor, Carissa Schlafer, of Carissa's Editorial Services, and my line editor, Ginny Ruths, Touchstone Publications, whose constructive feedback strengthened the story. In addition, any shortcomings that remain in the book after the editorial process are my own.

Chapter art generated by AI
Cover characters generated by AI
Cover design by Tea Jagodić.

ABOUT THE AUTHOR

Edgar spent the formative years of his life in Southern California, attending private schools. As a teen, he enjoyed reading horror and science fiction novels that explored utopian and dystopian ideas. He often wondered how a utopian society would come about. As a young adult, he noticed that most utopian and dystopian novels introduce readers to an unknown future without explaining its origin. Inspired by this, he wrote a story about a pre-utopian society on the cusp of becoming a great nation. Combining his love for fantasy, action, and suspense, he brings you an action-packed story that paves the path to a utopia. "Pay close attention," he says. "House of Broken Bones is a puzzle."

Edgar now lives in Ontario, California. He is retired and enjoys traveling and meeting with social clubs for karaoke, dining, and other fun activities.

X @EdgarJHern12748

OTHER TITLES
AS CLEAR AS NIGHT
(A SHORT STORY)

As Clear As Night is a gripping tale about Alex Blackwell, a man who gains extraordinary abilities after a freak accident. He discovers that he can vanish and reappear unharmed in a different location, a revelation that leads him into a world of crime and deception, testing the limits of his power and morality. After a series of unsuccessful criminal activities, he turns to his girlfriend, Stacey, for help. However, she firmly refuses, insisting that his abilities should be used for the benefit of humankind rather than corruption. When Stacey uncovers a dark secret about her own family, their lives become intertwined in a dangerous game of revenge and betrayal. As their paths collide, they must confront the consequences of their actions and decide whether to use their powers for good or succumb to the darkness.

Be sure to read the extra scene(s) in *House of Broken Bones*.

OTHER TITLES
THE CLOWN AND THE CAREGIVER
(A SHORT STORY)

Hurry, hurry, step right into the haunting world of *The Clown and The Caregiver*, where the glittering lights of Milagro Circus mask a sinister web of sabotage and terror. When a series of harrowing accidents plague the circus in Abilene, Texas, the performers point fingers at Daniel Dewhurst, the enigmatic carpet clown. Meanwhile, an ancient evil lurks within the reflection of a circus mirror, manipulating those who dare to look too closely. This darkly intertwined tale of betrayal, malevolence, and karmic justice will leave readers questioning the thin line between victim and villain.

Be sure to read the extra scene(s) in *House of Broken Bones*.

OTHER TITLES
HOUSE OF BROKEN BONES
(COMPLETE NOVEL)

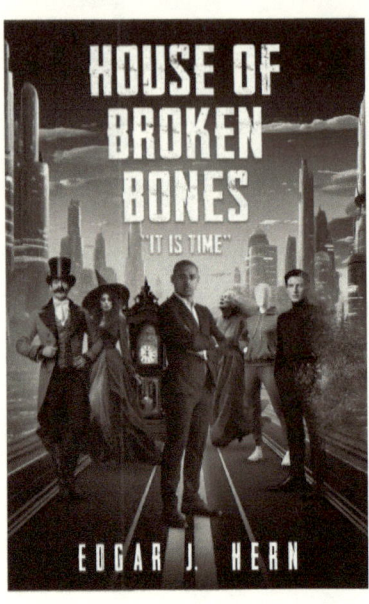

A collection of seven macabre and imaginative short stories that delve into the depths of human nature and the supernatural. From a man with the power to transport his physical body to a vengeful young woman who transforms into a wicked witch, these tales explore the extraordinary. A sinister circus plagued by sabotage, a grandfather clock with the ability to manipulate time, and a boy who breathes life into mannequins highlight the eerie and enigmatic. Additionally, a psychic girl fights to save the universe from implosion, and a provocative story examines the Senate's debate on eradicating money from society to combat the roots of evil. Each story is a piece of the puzzle, intricately interconnected to form a haunting tapestry.

www.ingramcontent.com/pod-product-compliance
Lightning Source LLC
Chambersburg PA
CBHW030553130626
46552CB00006B/2526